W9-BVM-922

PAL   Palmer, Diana.
           Heartbreaker.

$32.95

DATE			
		DISCARDED	

TLV

EXTENSION DEPARTMENT
ROCHESTER PUBLIC LIBRARY
115 SOUTH AVENUE
ROCHESTER, NY 14604-1896

AUG 2 3 2007

 BAKER & TAYLOR

HEARTBREAKER

**Center Point
Large Print**

**This Large Print Book carries the
Seal of Approval of N.A.V.H.**

HEARTBREAKER

DIANA PALMER

CENTER POINT PUBLISHING
THORNDIKE, MAINE

To Tara Gavin and Melissa Jeglinski, with love

This Center Point Large Print edition
is published in the year 2006 by arrangement with
Harlequin Enterprises Ltd.

Copyright © 2006 by Diana Palmer.

All rights reserved.

The text of this Large Print edition is unabridged. In other
aspects, this book may vary from the original edition.
Printed in the United States of America.
Set in 16-point Times New Roman type.

ISBN: 1-58547-841-5
ISBN 13: 978-1-58547-841-5

Library of Congress Cataloging-in-Publication Data

Palmer, Diana.
    Heartbreaker / Diana Palmer.--Center Point large print ed.
       p. cm.
    ISBN 1-58547-841-5 (lib. bdg. : alk. paper)
      1. Large type books. I. Title.

PS3566.A513H42 2006
813'.54--dc22

2006024083

One

It had been a grueling semester. Tellie Maddox had her history degree, but she was feeling betrayed. He hadn't shown up for her graduation exercises. Marge had, along with Dawn and Brandi, her two daughters. None of them were related to Tellie, who was orphaned many years ago, but they were as close to her as sisters. They'd cared enough to be here for her special day. J.B. hadn't. It was one more heartbreak in a whole series of them in Tellie's life that J.B. was responsible for.

She looked around her dorm room sadly, remembering how happy she'd been here for four years, sharing with Sandy Melton, a fellow history major. Sandy had already gone, off to England to continue her studies in medieval history. Tellie pushed back her short, wavy dark hair and sighed. Her pale green eyes searched for the last of her textbooks. She should take them to the campus bookstore, she supposed, and resell them. She was going to need every penny she could get to make it through the summer. When the fall semester began, in August, she was going to have to pay tuition again as she worked on her master's degree. She wanted to teach at college level. No chance of that, with just a bachelor's degree, unless she taught adult education as an adjunct member of staff.

Once she'd thought that one day J.B. might fall in love with her and want to marry her. Those hopeless dreams grew dimmer every day.

J. B. Hammock was Marge's brother. He'd rescued Tellie from a boy in the foster home where she'd been staying since her mother's death. Her mother had been the estranged wife of J.B.'s top horse wrangler, who'd later moved out of state and vanished. Tellie had gone to a foster home, despite Marge's objections, because J.B. said that a widow with two children to raise didn't need the complication of a teenager.

All that had changed with the attempted assault by another foster child in care with the same family. J.B. heard about it from a policeman who was one of his best friends. He swore out a warrant himself and had Tellie give a statement about what had happened. The boy, only thirteen at the time, was arrested and subsequently sent to juvenile hall. Tellie had slugged the boy when he tried to remove her blouse and sat on him until the family heard her yelling. Even at such a young age, Tellie was fearless. It had helped that the boy was half her size and half-drunk.

J.B. had jerked Tellie right out of the foster home the night the boy was arrested. He'd taken her straight to Marge for sanctuary. Marge had loved her almost at once. Most people did love Tellie. She was honest and sweet and generous with her time, and she wasn't afraid of hard work. Even at the age of fourteen, she'd taken charge of the kitchen and Dawn and Brandi. The sisters were nine and ten at the time respectively. They'd loved having an older girl in the house. Marge's job as a Realtor kept her on the road at all sorts of odd hours. But she could depend on Tellie to keep the girls in school clothes and help with their homework. She was a born baby-sitter.

Tellie had doted on J.B. He was very rich, and very temperamental. He owned hundreds of acres of prime ranch land near Jacobsville, where he raised purebred Santa Gertrudis cattle and entertained the rich and famous at his hundred-year-old rancho. He had a fabulous French chef in residence, along with a housekeeper named Nell who could singe the feathers off a duck with her temper at ten paces. Nell ran the house, and J.B., to an extent. He knew famous politicians, and movie stars, and foreign royalty from his days as a rodeo champion. He had impeccable manners, a legacy from his Spanish grandmother, and wealth from his British grandfather, who had been a peer of the realm. J.B.'s roots were European, despite his very American cattle operation.

But he did intimidate people. Locally he was known more for chasing Ralph Barrows off his place on foot, wielding a replica fantasy sword from the Lord of the Rings movie trilogy. Barrows had gotten drunk and shot J.B.'s favorite German shepherd for growling at him and barking when he tried to sneak into the bunkhouse in the small hours of the morning during roundup. Drinking wasn't allowed on the ranch. And nobody hurt an animal there. J.B. couldn't get to the key to his gun cabinet fast enough, so he grabbed the sword from its wall display and struck out for the bunkhouse the minute his foreman told him what was going on. The dog recovered, although it limped badly. Barrows hadn't been seen since.

J.B. wasn't really a social animal, despite the grand parties he threw at the ranch. He kept to himself, except for the numerous gorgeous women he squired around in his private jet. He had a nasty temper and the arrogance of position and wealth. Tellie was closer to him than almost anyone, even Marge, because she'd taken charge of him when she was fourteen and he went on a legendary drunk after his father died. It was Tellie who'd made Marge drive her to J.B.'s place when Nell called in a panic and said that J.B. was wrecking the den and the computers. It was Tellie who'd set him down, calmed him, and made cinnamon coffee for him to help sober him up.

J.B. tolerated her interventions over the years. He was like her property, her private male. Nobody dared to say that, of course, not even Tellie. But she was possessive of him and, as she grew older, she became jealous of the women who passed through his life in such numbers. She tried not to let it show. Invariably, though, it did.

When she was eighteen, one of his girlfriends had made an unkind remark to Tellie, who'd flared back at her that J.B. wouldn't keep *her* around for much longer if she was going to be rude to his family! After the girl left, J.B. had it out with Tellie, his green eyes flaming like emeralds, his thick black hair almost standing up straight on his head with bad temper. Tellie didn't own him, he reminded her, and if she didn't stop trying to possess him, she'd be out on her ear. She wasn't even part of his family, he'd added cruelly. She had no right

8

whatsoever to make any claims on his life.

She'd shot back that his girlfriends were all alike—long-legged, big-breasted, pretty girls with the brains of bats! He'd looked at her small breasts and remarked that she certainly wouldn't fit that description.

She'd slapped him. It was involuntary and she was immediately sorry. But before she could take it back, he'd jerked her against his tall, lean body and kissed her in a way that still made her knees weak four years later. It had been meant, she was sure, as a punishment. But her mouth had opened weakly under his in a silent protest, and the tiny movement had kindled a shudder in the muscular body so close to hers.

He'd backed her up against the sofa and crushed her down on it, under the length of him. The kiss had grown hard, insistent, passionate. His big, lean hand had found her breast under her blouse, and she'd panicked. The sensations he caused made her push at him and fight to get free.

She jerked her mind back to the present. J.B. had torn himself away from her, in an even worse temper than before. His eyes had blazed down at her, as if she'd done something unforgivable. Furious, he'd told her to get out of his life and stay out. She was due to leave for college the same week, and he hadn't even said goodbye. He'd ignored her from that day onward.

Holidays had come and gone. Slowly tensions had lessened between them, but J.B. had made sure that they were never alone again. He'd given her presents for her birthday and Christmas, but they were always impersonal ones, like computer hardware or software, or biography and history books that he knew she liked. She'd given him ties. In fact, she'd given him the same exact tie for every birthday and every Christmas present. She'd found a closeout special and bought two boxes of identical ties. She was set for life, she reasoned, for presents for J.B. Marge had remarked on the odd and monotonous present, but J.B. himself said nothing at all. Well, he said thank you every time he opened a present from Tellie, but he said nothing more. Presumably he'd given the ties away. He never wore one. Tellie hadn't expected that he would. They were incredibly ugly. Yellow, with a putrid green dragon with red eyes. She still had enough left for ten more years . . .

"Are you ready, Tellie?" Marge called from the door.

She was like her brother, tall and dark-haired, but her eyes were brown where J.B.'s were green. Marge had a sweet nature, and she wasn't violent. She had a livewire personality. Everybody loved her. She was long widowed and had never looked at another man. Love, she often told Tellie, for some people was undying, even if one lost the partner. She would never find anyone else as wonderful as her late husband. She had no interest in trying.

"I just have a couple more blouses to pack," Tellie said with a smile.

Dawn and Brandi wandered around her dorm room curiously.

"You'll do this one day, yourselves," Tellie assured them.

"Not me," Dawn, the youngest, at sixteen, replied

with a grin. "I'm going to be a cattle baron like Uncle J.B. when I get through agricultural college."

"I'm going to be an attorney," Brandi, who would be a senior in the fall at seventeen, said with a smile. "I want to help poor people."

"She can already bargain me into anything," Marge said with an amused wink at Tellie.

"Me, too," Tellie had to admit. "She's still got my favorite jacket, and I never even got to wear it once."

"It looks much better on me," Brandi assured her. "Red just isn't your color."

A lot she knew, Tellie thought, because every time she thought about J.B., she saw red.

Marge watched Tellie pack her suitcase with a somber expression. "He really did have an emergency at the ranch," she told Tellie gently. "The big barn caught fire. They had fire departments from all over Jacobs County out there putting it out."

"I'm sure he would have come, if he'd been able," Tellie replied politely. She didn't believe it. J.B. hadn't shown any interest in her at all in recent years. He'd avoided her whenever possible. Perhaps the ties had driven him nuts and he'd torched the barn himself, thinking of it as a giant yellow dragon tie. The thought amused her, and she laughed.

"What are you laughing about?" Marge teased.

"I was thinking maybe J.B.'s gone off his rocker and started seeing yellow dragon ties everywhere . . ."

Marge chuckled. "It wouldn't surprise me. Those ties are just awful, Tellie, really!"

"I think they suit him," Tellie said with irrepressible humor. "I'm sure that he's going to wear one eventually."

Marge started to speak and apparently thought better of it. "Well, I wouldn't hold my breath waiting," she said instead.

"Who's the flavor of the month?" Tellie wondered aloud.

Marge lifted an eyebrow. She knew what Tellie meant, all too well. She despaired of her brother ever getting serious about a woman again. "He's dating one of the Kingstons's cousins, from Fort Worth. She was a runner-up for Miss Texas."

Tellie wasn't surprised. J.B. had a passion for beautiful blondes. Over the years, he'd escorted his share of movie starlets. Tellie, with her ordinary face and figure, was hardly on a par to compete with such beauties.

"They're just display models," Marge whispered wickedly, so that her daughters didn't hear her.

Tellie burst out laughing. "Oh, Marge, what would I do without you?"

Marge shrugged. "It's us against the men of the world," she pointed out. "Even my brother qualifies as the enemy from time to time." She paused. "Don't they give you a CD of the graduation exercises?"

"Yes, along with my diploma," Tellie agreed. "Why?"

"I say we get the boys to rope J.B. to his easy chair in the den and make him watch the CD for twenty-four straight hours," she suggested. "Revenge is sweet!"

"He'd just go to sleep during the commencement

speech," Tellie sighed. "And I wouldn't blame him. I almost did myself."

"Shame on you! The speaker was a famous politician!"

"Famously boring," Brandi remarked with a wicked grin.

"Notice how furiously everybody applauded when he stopped speaking," Dawn agreed.

"You two have been hanging out with me for too long," Tellie observed. "You're picking up all my bad habits."

They both hugged her. "We love you, bad habits and all," they said. "Congratulations on your degree!"

"You did very well indeed," Marge echoed. "Magna cum laude, no less! I'm proud of you."

"Honor graduates don't have social lives, Mother," Brandi pointed out. "No wonder she made such good grades. She spent every weekend in the dorm, studying!"

"Not every weekend," Tellie muttered. "There was that archaeology field trip . . ."

"With the geek squad." Dawn yawned.

"They weren't all geeks," she reminded them. "Anyway, I like digging up old things."

"Then you should have gotten your degree in archaeology instead of history," Brandi said.

She chuckled. "I'll be digging up old documents instead of old relics," she said. "It will be a cleaner job, at least."

"When do you start your master's degree work?" Marge asked.

"Fall semester," she replied, smiling. "I thought I'd take the summer off and spend a little time with you guys. I've already lined up a job working for the Ballenger brothers at their feedlot while Calhoun and Abby take a cruise to Greece with the boys. I guess all those summers following J.B. and his veterinarian around the ranch finally paid off. At least I know enough about feeding out cattle to handle the paperwork!"

"Lucky Calhoun and Abby. Wow," Dawn said on a sigh. "I'd love to get a three-month vacation!"

"Wouldn't we all," Tellie agreed wistfully. "In my case, a job is a vacation from all the studying! Biology was so hard!"

"We don't get to dissect things anymore at our school," Brandi said. "Everybody's afraid of blood these days."

"With good reason, I'm sorry to say," Marge mused.

"We don't get to do dissections, either," Tellie told her with a smile. "We had a rat on a dissecting board and we all got to use it for identification purposes. It was so nice that we had an air-conditioned lab!"

The girls made faces.

"Speaking of labs," Marge interrupted, "who wants a nice hamburger?"

"Nobody dissects cows, Mom," Brandi informed her.

"We can dissect the hamburger," Tellie suggested, "and identify the part of the cow it came from."

"It came from a steer, not a cow," Marge said wryly. "You could use a refresher course in Ranching 101, Tellie."

They all knew who'd be teaching it at home, and that was a sore spot. Tellie's smile faded. "I expect I'll get all the information I need working from Justin at the feedlot."

"They've got some handsome new cowboys working for them," Marge said with sparkling eyes. "One's an ex–Green Beret who grew up on a ranch in West Texas."

Tellie shrugged one shoulder. "I'm not sure I want to meet any men. I've still got three years of study to get my master's degree so that I can start teaching history in college."

"You can teach now, can't you?" Dawn asked.

"I can teach adult education," Tellie replied. "But I have to have at least a master's degree to teach at the college level, and a Ph.D. is preferred."

"Why don't you want to teach little kids?" Brandi asked curiously.

Tellie grinned. "Because you two hooligans destroyed all my illusions about sweet little kids," she replied, and ducked when Brandi threw a pillow at her.

"We were such sweet little kids," Dawn said belligerently. "You better say we were, or else, Tellie!"

"Or else what?" she replied.

Dawn wiggled her eyebrows. "Or else I'll burn the potatoes. It's my night to cook supper at home."

"Don't pay any attention to her, dear," Marge said. "She always burns the potatoes."

"Oh, Mom!" the teenager wailed.

Tellie just laughed. But her heart wasn't in the word-play. She was miserable because J.B. had missed her graduation, and nothing was going to make up for that.

Marge's house was on the outskirts of Jacobsville, about six miles from the big ranch that had been in her and J.B.'s family for three generations. It was a friendly little house with a bay window out front and a small front porch with a white swing. All around it were the flowers that Marge planted obsessively. It was May, and everything was blooming. Every color in the rainbow graced the small yard, including a small rose garden with an arch that was Marge's pride and joy. These were antique roses, not hybrids, and they had scents that were like perfume.

"I'd forgotten all over again how beautiful it was," Tellie said on a sigh.

"Howard loved it, too," Marge said, her dark eyes soft with memories for an instant as she looked around the lush, clipped lawn that led to the stepping stone walkway that led to the front porch.

"I never met him," Tellie said. "But he must have been a lovely person."

"He was," Marge agreed, her eyes sad as she recalled her husband.

"Look, it's Uncle J.B.!" Dawn cried, pointing to the narrow paved road that led up to the dirt driveway of Marge's house.

Tellie felt every muscle in her body contract. She turned around as the sporty red Jaguar slid to a halt, throwing up clouds of yellow dust. The door opened and J.B. climbed out.

He was tall and lean, with jet-black hair and dark green eyes. His cheekbones were high, his mouth thin. He had big ears and big feet. But he was so masculine that women were drawn to him like magnets. He had a sensuality in his walk that made Tellie's heart skip.

"Where the hell have you been?" he growled as he joined them. "I looked everywhere for you until I finally gave up and drove back home!"

"What do you mean, where were we?" Marge exclaimed. "We were at Tellie's graduation. Not that you could be bothered to show up . . . !"

"I was across the stadium from you," J.B. said harshly. "I didn't see you until it was over. By the time I got through the crowd and out of the parking lot, you'd left the dorm and headed down here."

"You came to my graduation?" Tellie asked, in a husky, soft tone.

He turned, glaring at her. His eyes were large, framed by thick black lashes, deep-set and biting. "We had a fire at the barn. I was late. Do you think I'd miss some-thing so important as your college graduation?" he added angrily, although his eyes evaded hers.

Her heart lifted, against her will. He didn't want her. She was like a second sister to him. But any contact with him made her tingle with delight. She couldn't help the radiance that lit up her plain face and made it pretty.

He glanced around him irritably and caught Tellie's

hand, sending a thrill all the way to her heart. "Come here," he said, drawing her to the car with him.

He put her in the passenger side, closed the door and went around to get in beside her. He reached into the console between the bucket seats and pulled out a gold-wrapped box. He handed it to her.

She took it, her eyes surprised. "For me?"

"For no one else," he drawled, smiling faintly. "Go on. Look."

She tore open the wrapping. It was a jeweler's box, but far too big to be a ring. She opened the box and stared at it blankly.

He frowned. "What's the matter? Don't you like it?"

"It" was a Mickey Mouse watch with a big face and a gaudy red band. She knew what it meant, too. It meant that his secretary, Miss Jarrett, who hated being delegated to buy presents for him, had finally lost her cool. She thought J.B. was buying jewelry for one of his women, and Miss Jarrett was showing him that he'd better get his own gifts from now on.

It hurt Tellie, who knew that J.B. shopped for Marge and the girls himself. He never delegated that chore to underlings. But, then, Tellie wasn't family.

"It's . . . very nice," she stammered, aware that the silence had gone on a little too long for politeness.

She took the watch out of the box and he saw it for the first time.

Blistering range language burst from his chiseled lips before he could stop himself. Then his high cheekbones went dusky because he couldn't very well admit to

Tellie that he hadn't bothered to go himself to get her a present. He'd kill Jarrett, though, he promised himself.

"It's the latest thing," he said with deliberate nonchalance.

"I love it. Really." She put it on her wrist. She did love it, because he'd given it to her. She'd have loved a dead rat in a box if it had come from J.B., because she had no pride.

He pursed his lips, the humor of the situation finally getting through to him. His green eyes twinkled. "You'll be the only graduate on your block to wear one," he pointed out.

She laughed. It changed her face, made her radiant. "Thanks, J.B.," she said.

He tugged her as close as the console would allow, and his eyes shifted to her soft, parted lips. "You can do better than that," he murmured wickedly, and bent.

She lifted her face, closed her eyes, savored the warm, tender pressure of his hard mouth on her soft one.

He stiffened. "No, you don't," he whispered roughly when she kept her lips firmly closed. He caught her cheek in one big, lean hand and pressed, gently, just enough to open her mouth. He bent and caught it, hard, pressing her head back against the padded seat with the force of it.

Tellie went under in a daze, loving the warm, hard insistence of his mouth in the silence of the little car. She sighed and a husky little moan escaped her taut throat.

He lifted his head. Dark green eyes probed her own, narrow and hot and full of frustrated desire.

"And here we are again," he said roughly.

She swallowed. "J.B. . . ."

He put his thumb against her soft lips to stop the words. "I told you, there's no future in this, Tellie," he said, his voice hard and cold. "I don't want any woman on a permanent basis. Ever. I'm a bachelor, and I mean to stay that way. Understand?"

"But I didn't say anything," she protested.

"The hell you didn't," he bit off. He put her back in her seat and opened his car door.

She went with him back to Marge and the girls, showing off her new watch. "Look, isn't it neat?" she asked.

"I want one, too!" Brandi exclaimed.

"You don't graduate until next year, darling," Marge reminded her daughter.

"Well, I want one then," she repeated stubbornly.

"I'll keep that in mind," J.B. promised. He smiled, but it wasn't in his eyes. "Congratulations again, tidbit," he told Tellie. "I've got to go. I have a hot date tonight."

He was looking straight at Tellie as he said it. She only smiled.

"Thanks for the watch," she told him.

He shrugged. "It does suit you," he remarked enigmatically. "See you, girls."

He got into the sports car and roared away.

"I'd really love one of those," Brandi remarked on a sigh as she watched it leave.

Marge lifted Tellie's wrist and glared at the watch. "That was just mean," she said under her breath.

Tellie smiled sadly. "He sent Jarrett after it. He always has her buy presents for everybody except you and the girls. She obviously thought it was for one of his platinum blondes, and she got this out of spite."

"Yes, I figured that out all by myself," Marge replied, glowering. "But it's you who got hurt, not J.B."

"It's Jarrett who'll get hurt when he goes back to work," Tellie said on a sigh. "Poor old lady."

"She'll have him for breakfast," Marge said. "And she should."

"He does like sharp older women, doesn't he?" Tellie remarked on the way into the house. "He's got Nell at the house, taking care of things there, and she could scorch leather in a temper."

"Nell's a fixture," Marge said, smiling. "I don't know what J.B. and I would have done without her when we were kids. There was just Dad and us. Mom died when we were very young. Dad was never affectionate."

"Is that why J.B.'s such a rounder?" Tellie wondered.

As usual, Marge clammed up. "We don't ever talk about that," she said. "It isn't a pretty story, and J.B. hates even the memory."

"Nobody ever told me," Tellie persisted.

Marge gave her a gentle smile. "Nobody ever will, pet, unless it's J.B. himself."

"I know when that will be," Tellie sighed. "When they're wearing overcoats in hell."

"Exactly," Marge agreed warmly.

That night, they were watching a movie on television when the phone rang. Marge answered it. She came back in a few minutes, wincing.

"It's Jarrett," she told Tellie. "She wants to talk to you."

"How bad was it?" Tellie asked.

Marge made a face.

Tellie picked up the phone. "Hello?"

"Tellie? It's Nan Jarrett. I just want to apologize . . ."

"It's not your fault, Miss Jarrett," Tellie said at once. "It really is a cute watch. I love it."

"But it was your college graduation present," the older woman wailed. "I thought it was for one of those idiot blond floozies he carts around, and it made me mad that he didn't even care enough about them to buy a present himself." She realized what she'd just said and cleared her throat. "Not that I think he didn't care enough about *you,* of course . . . !"

"Obviously he doesn't," Tellie said through her teeth.

"Well, you wouldn't be so sure of that if you'd been here when he got back into the office just before quitting time," came the terse reply. "I have never heard such language in my life, even from him!"

"He was just mad that he got caught," Tellie said.

"He said it was one of the most special days of your life and I screwed it up," Miss Jarrett said miserably.

"He'd already done that by not showing up for my graduation," Tellie said, about to mention that none of them had seen him in the stands and thought he hadn't shown up.

"Oh, you know about that?" came the unexpected reply. "He told us all to remember he'd been fighting a fire in case it came up. He had a meeting with an out-of-town cattle buyer and his daughter. He forgot all about the commencement exercises."

Tellie's heart broke in two. "Yes," she said, fighting tears, "well, nobody's going to say anything. None of us, certainly."

"Certainly. He gets away with murder."

"I wish I could," Tellie said under her breath. "Thanks for calling, Miss Jarrett. It was nice of you."

"I just wanted you to know how bad I felt," the older woman said with genuine regret. "I wouldn't have hurt your feelings for the world."

"I know that."

"Well, happy graduation, anyway."

"Thanks."

Tellie hung up. She went back into the living room smiling. She was never going to tell them the truth about her graduation. But she knew that she'd never forget.

Two

Tellie had learned to hide her deepest feelings over the years, so Marge and the girls didn't notice any change in her. There was one. She was tired of waiting for J.B. to wake up and notice that she was around. She'd finally realized that she meant nothing to him. Well, maybe she was a sort of adopted relative for whom he

23

had an occasional fondness. But his recent behavior had finally drowned her fondest hopes of anything serious. She was going to convince her stupid heart to stop aching for him, if it killed her.

Five days later, on a Monday, she walked into Calhoun and Justin Ballenger's office at their feedlot, ready for work.

Justin, Calhoun's elder brother, gave her a warm welcome. He was tall, whipcord lean, with gray-sprinkled black hair and dark eyes. He and his wife, Shelby—who was a direct descendant of the founder of Jacobsville, old John Jacobs—had three sons. They'd been married for a long time, like Calhoun and Abby. J. D. Langley's wife, Fay, had been working for the Ballengers as Calhoun's secretary, but a rough pregnancy had forced her to give it up temporarily. That was why Tellie was in such demand.

"You'll manage," Justin's secretary, Ellie, assured her with a smile. "We're not so rushed now as we are in the early spring and autumn. It's just nice and routine. I'll introduce you to the men later on. For now, let me show you what you'll be doing."

"Sorry you have to give up your own vacation for this," Justin said apologetically.

"Listen, I can't afford a vacation yet," she assured him with a grin. "I'm a lowly college student. I have to pay my tuition for three more years. I'm the one who's grateful for the job."

Justin shrugged. "You know as much about cattle as Abby and Shelby do," he said, which was high praise,

24

since both were actively involved in the feedlot operation and the local cattlemen's association. "You're welcome here."

"Thanks," she said, and meant it.

"Thank you," he replied, and left them to it.

The work wasn't that difficult. Most of it dealt with spreadsheets, various programs that kept a daily tally on the number of cattle from each client and the feeding regimen they followed. It was involved and required a lot of concentration, and the phones seemed to ring constantly. It wasn't all clients asking about cattle. Many of the calls were from prospective customers. Others were from buyers who had contracted to take possession of certain lots of cattle when they were fed out. There were also calls from various organizations to which the Ballenger brothers belonged, and even a few from state and federal legislators. A number of them came from overseas, where the brothers had investments. Tellie found it all fascinating.

It took her a few days to get into the routine of things, and to get to know the men who worked at the feedlot. She could identify them all by face, if not by name.

One of them was hard to miss. He was the ex–Green Beret, a big, tall man from El Paso named Grange. If he had a first name, Tellie didn't hear anyone use it. He had straight black hair and dark brown eyes, an olive complexion and a deep, sexy voice. He liked Tellie on sight and made no secret of it. It amused Justin, because

Grange hadn't shown any interest in anything in the weeks he'd been working on the place. It was the first spark of life the man had displayed.

He told Tellie, who looked surprised.

"He seems like a friendly man," she stammered.

He lifted a dark eyebrow. "The first day he worked here, one of the boys short-sheeted his bed. He turned on the lights, looked around the room, dumped one of the other men out of a bunk bed and threw him head-first into the yard."

"Was it the right man?" Tellie asked, wide-eyed.

"It was. Nobody knew how he figured it out, and he never said. But the boys walk wide around him. Especially since he threw that big knife he carries at a sidewinder that crawled too close to the bunkhouse. Cag Hart has a reputation for that sort of accuracy with a Bowie, but he used to be the only one. Grange is a mystery."

She was intrigued. "What did he do, before he came here?"

"Nobody knows. Nobody asks, either," he added with a grin.

"Was he stationed overseas, in the army?"

"Nobody knows that, either. The 411 is that he was in the Green Berets, but he's never said he was. Puzzling guy. But he's a hard worker. And he's honest." He pursed his lips and his dark eyes twinkled. "And he never takes a drink. Ever."

She whistled. "Well!"

"Anyway, you'd better not agree to any dates with

him until J.B. checks him out," Justin said. "I don't want J.B. on the wrong side of me." He grinned. "We feed out a lot of cattle for him," he added, making it clear that he wasn't afraid of J.B.

"J.B. doesn't tell me who I can date," she said, hurting as she remembered how little she meant to Marge's big brother.

"Just the same, I don't know anything about Grange, and I'm sort of responsible for you while you're here, even though you're legally an adult," Justin said quietly. "Get the picture?"

She grimaced. "I do. Okay, I'll make sure I don't let him bulldoze me into anything."

"That's the spirit," he said with a grin. "I'm not saying he's a bad man, mind you. I just don't know a lot about him. He's always on time, does his job and a bit more, and gets along fairly well with other people. But he mostly keeps to himself when he's not working. He's not a sociable sort."

"I feel somewhat that way, myself," she sighed.

"Join the club. Things going okay for you otherwise? The job's not too much?"

"The job's great," she said, smiling. "I'm really enjoying this."

"Good. We're glad to have you here. Anything you need, let me know."

"Sure thing. Thanks!"

She told Marge and the girls about Grange. They were amused.

"He obviously has good taste," Marge mused, "if he likes you."

Tellie chuckled as she rinsed dishes and put them in the dishwasher. "It's not mutual," she replied. "He's a little scary, in a way."

"What do you mean? Does he seem violent or something?" Brandi wanted to know.

Tellie paused with a dish in her hand and frowned. "I don't know. I'm not afraid of him, really. It's just that he has that sort of effect on people. Kind of like Cash Grier," she added.

"He's calmed down a bit since Tippy Moore came to stay with him after her kidnapping," Marge said. "Rumor is that he may marry her."

"She's really pretty, even with those cuts on her face," Dawn remarked from the kitchen table, where she was arranging cloth for a quilt she meant to make. "They say somebody real mean is after her, and that's why she's here. Mrs. Jewell stays at the house at night. A stickler for convention, is our police chief."

"Good for him," Marge said. "A few people need to be conventional, or society is going to fall."

Brandi looked at her sister and rolled her eyes. "Here we go again with the lecture."

"Uncle J.B. isn't conventional," Dawn reminded her mother. "He had that football team cheerleader staying at his house for almost a month. And his new girlfriend was a runner-up Miss Texas, and she spends weekends with him . . ."

Tellie's hands were shaking. Dawn grimaced and

looked at her mother helplessly.

Dawn got up and hugged Tellie from behind. "I'm sorry, Tellie," she said with obvious remorse.

Tellie patted the hands around her waist. "Just because I'm a hopeless case, doesn't mean you have to walk on eggshells around me," she assured the younger woman. "We all know that J.B. isn't ever going to get married. And even if he did, it would be some beautiful, sophisticated—"

"You hush," Marge broke in. "You're pretty. Besides, it's what's inside that counts. Beauty doesn't last. Character does."

"Her stock phrase," Brandi said with a grin. "But she's right, Tellie. I think you're beautiful."

"Thanks, guys," Tellie murmured.

She went back to her task, and the conversation became general.

The next day Grange came right up to Tellie's desk and stood staring down at her, wordlessly, until she was forced to look up at him.

"They say that you live with J. B. Hammock's sister, Marge," he said.

She was totally confounded by the question. She stared at him blankly. "Excuse me?"

He shrugged, looking uncomfortable. "I didn't come to Jacobsville by accident," he said, glancing around as Justin came out of his office and gave him a faint glower. "Have lunch with me," he added. "It's not a pass. I just want to talk to you."

If it was a line, it was a good one. "Okay," she said.

"I'll pick you up at noon." He tipped his wide-brimmed hat, nodded toward Justin, and went back out to the feedlot.

Justin went straight to Tellie. "Trouble?" he asked.

"Well, no," she said. "He wants to talk to me about Marge, apparently."

His eyebrows arched. "That's a new one."

"He was serious. He wants me to have lunch with him." She grinned. "He can't do much to me over a hamburger in town."

"Good point. Okay, but watch your step. Like I said," he added, "he's an unknown quantity."

"I'll do that," she promised.

Barbara's Café in town was the local hot spot for lunch. Just about everybody ate there when they wanted something home cooked. There were other places, such as the Chinese and Mexican restaurants, and the pizza place. But Barbara's had a sort of Texas atmosphere that appealed even to tourists.

Today it was crowded. Grange got them a table and ordered steak and potatoes for himself, leaving Tellie to get what she wanted. They'd already agreed they were going Dutch. So he must have meant it, about it not being a date.

"My people were all dead, and Marge and J.B. took me in," Tellie said when they'd given their orders to the waitress. She didn't add why. "I've known the Hammocks since I was a child, but I was fourteen when I went to live with Marge and her girls. She was widowed by then."

"Are you and J.B. close?" he queried, placing his hat in an empty chair.

"No," she said flatly. She didn't elaborate. She started to get the feeling that it was not Marge he wanted information on.

His dark eyes narrowed as he studied her. "What do you know about his past?" he asked.

Her heart jumped. "You mean, generally?"

"I mean," he added with flaming eyes, "do you know anything about the woman he tried to marry when he was twenty-one?"

She felt suddenly cold, and didn't know why. "What woman?" she asked, her voice sounded hoarse and choked.

He looked around them to make sure they weren't being overheard. He lifted his coffee cup and held it in his big, lean hands. "His father threatened to cut him off without a cent if he went through with the wedding. He was determined to do it. He withdrew his savings from the bank—he was of legal age, so he could—and he picked her up at her house and they took off to Louisiana. He was going to marry her there. He thought nobody could find them. But his father did."

This was fascinating stuff. Nobody had said anything to her about it, certainly not J.B. "Did they get married?"

His face tautened. "His father waited until J.B. went out to see about the marriage license. He went in and

31

talked to the woman. He told her that if she married J.B., he'd turn in her brother, who was fourteen and had gotten mixed up with a gang that dealt in distribution of crack cocaine. There had been a death involved in a drug deal gone bad. The boy hadn't participated, but he could be implicated as an accessory. J.B.'s father had a private detective document everything. He told the woman her brother would go to prison for twenty years."

She grimaced. "Did J.B. know?"

"I don't know," he said uncomfortably. "I came here to find out."

"But what did she do?"

"What could she do?" he asked curtly. "She loved her brother. He was the only family she had. She loved Hammock. She really loved him."

"But she loved her brother more?"

He nodded. His whole face clenched. "She didn't tell Hammock what his father had done. She did tell her father."

"Did he do anything?"

"He couldn't. They were poor. There was nothing he could do. Well, he did get her brother to leave the gang when she killed herself. It was all that saved him from prison."

She was hanging on his every word. "What about the woman?"

"She was already clinically depressed," he said in an odd monotone, toying with his fork, not looking at her. He seemed to be far away, in time. "She knew that she could never be with Hammock, that his father would make sure of it. She couldn't see any future without him." His fingers tightened on the fork. "She found the pistol her brother had hidden in his room. She shot herself. She died instantly."

The iced tea went all over the tablecloth. Tellie quickly uprighted the glass and grabbed at napkins to mop up the flow. Barbara, seeing the accident, came forward with a tea cloth.

"There, there, we all spill things," she told Tellie with a smile. "Right as rain," she added when she'd mopped the oilcloth-covered table. "I'll bring you a new glass. Unsweetened?"

Tellie nodded, still reeling from what Grange had told her. "Yes. Thanks."

"No problem," Barbara said, smiling at them both as she left.

"You really didn't know, did you?" Grange asked quietly. "I'm sorry. I don't want to hurt you. It's not your fault."

She swallowed, hard. It all made sense. Why J.B. never got serious about a woman. Why he refused to think of marriage. He'd had that death on his conscience all his life, when it wasn't even his fault, not really. It was his father's.

"His father must have been a horror," she said unsteadily.

Grange stared at her. "Have been?" he queried.

She nodded. "He died in a nursing home the year I moved in with Marge," she said. "He'd had a stroke and he never fully recovered from it. It left him in a vegetative state. J.B. paid to keep him in the facility."

"And the old man's wife?"

"She died long before I lived with Marge. I don't know how."

He looked odd. "I see."

"How do you know all this?" she wondered.

"Her brother is a friend of mine," he told her. "He was curious about the old man. I needed a job, and this one at the feedlot came available. I like Texas. It was close enough that I could find out about old man Hammock for him."

"Well, now you know," she said, trying not to let the trauma show in her face.

He frowned. His hard face went even harder. He stared down into his coffee cup. "I didn't realize it would have such an impact on you."

"J.B. is like an older brother to me," she told him, lying through her teeth. "But nobody ever told me why he plays the field like he does, why he won't consider ever getting married. I thought he just liked being a bachelor. I guess he blames himself for what happened, don't you think?" she added, surprising an odd look on Grange's face. "Even though it was his father who did the real damage, J.B. surely realized that if he'd never gotten mixed up with the poor woman, she'd still be alive."

He winced. "You don't pull your punches, do you?"

"It's the truth, isn't it?" she added thoughtfully.

"So he doesn't want to get married," he said after a minute.

She nodded. "He has lots of girlfriends. The new one

was a runner-up in the Miss Texas pageant."

He didn't even seem to be listening. He finished his steak and sat back to sip cold coffee.

Barbara came around with Tellie's new glass of tea and the coffeepot. She warmed Grange's in his cup.

"Thanks," he said absently.

She grinned at him. "No problem. You're new here, aren't you?"

"I am," he confessed. "I work for Justin and Calhoun, at the feedlot."

"Lucky you," she said. "They're good people."

He nodded.

She glanced at Tellie. "How's Marge?"

There was something in the question that made Tellie stare at her. "She's fine. Why?"

Barbara grimaced. "It's nothing, really."

"Tell me," Tellie persisted. It was her day for learning things about people she thought she knew.

"Well, she had a dizzy spell the last time she ate lunch here. She fell into one of the tables." She sighed. "I wondered if she ever had a checkup. Just to make sure. I never knew Marge to have dizzy spells."

"Me, either," Tellie said, frowning. "But I'll find out," she promised.

"Don't tell her I told you," Barbara said firmly. "She can light fires when she's mad, just like J.B."

"I'll ask her gently, I promise," Tellie said, smiling. "She won't get mad."

"If you do, you'll eat burned hamburgers forever," Barbara told her.

"That's just mean," she told the older woman, who grinned and went back to the kitchen.

"Well, it's your day for revelations, apparently," Grange observed.

"I don't think I know anybody anymore," she agreed.

"Listen, don't tell Hammock's sister about any of this," he said suddenly. "I'm not here to cause trouble. I just wanted to find out what became of the old man." His eyes darkened. "I suppose J.B. knew what his father did?"

"I have no way of knowing," she said uneasily.

He put cream into his hot coffee. He drew in a long breath. "I'm sorry if I shattered any illusions."

He had. He'd just put the final nail in the coffin of her dreams. But that wasn't his fault. Tellie always felt that people came into your life for a reason. She forced a smile. "I don't have illusions about J.B.," she told him. "I've seen all his bad character traits firsthand."

He searched her green eyes. "One of the boys said you're in college."

She nodded. "I start master's work in the fall."

"What's your subject?"

"History. My field is Native American studies. I hope to teach at the college level when I finally get my master's degree."

"Why not teach grammar school or middle or high school?" he wondered.

"Because little kids walk all over me," she said flatly. "Marge's girls had me on my ear the first six months I lived with them, because I couldn't say no.

36

I'd make a lousy elementary school teacher."

He smiled faintly. "I'll bet the girls loved you."

She nodded, smiling back. "They're very special."

He finished his coffee. "We'll have to do this again sometime," he began, just as the café door opened and J.B. walked in.

J.B.'s eyes slithered over the patrons until he spotted Tellie. He walked to the table where Tellie and Grange were sitting and stared down at Grange with pure venom. His eyes were blistering hot.

"What are you doing here in Jacobsville?" he asked Grange.

The other man studied him coolly. "Working. Tellie and I are having lunch together."

"That doesn't answer the question," J.B. replied, and he'd never sounded more menacing.

Grange sipped coffee with maddening calm. "So the old man did finally tell you what happened, did he?" he asked with a sudden, piercing glance. "He told you what he said to my sister?"

J.B.'s big fists clenched at his side. He aged in seconds. "Not while he was alive. He left a letter with his will."

"At least you had time to get used to the idea, didn't you?" Grange asked icily. "I found out three weeks ago!" He forced his deep voice back into calmer channels and took a deep breath. "Care to guess how I felt when my father finally told *me,* on his death bed?"

J.B. seemed to calm down himself. "You didn't know?" he asked.

"No," Grange said harshly. "No, I didn't know! If I had . . . !"

J.B. seemed suddenly aware of Tellie's rapt interest and he seemed to go pale under his tan. He saw her new knowledge of him in her paleness, in her suddenly averted face. He looked at Grange. "You told her, didn't you?" he demanded.

The other man stood up. He and J.B. were the same height, although Grange seemed huskier, more muscular. J.B. had a range rider's lean physique.

"Secrets are dangerous, Hammock," Grange said, and he didn't back down an inch. "There were things I wanted to know that I'd never have heard from you."

"Such as?" J.B. asked in a curt tone.

Grange looked at him openly, aware that other diners were watching them. His shoulders moved in a curious jerk. "I came here with another whole idea in mind, but your young friend here shot me in the foot. I didn't realize that you were as much a victim as I was. I thought you put your father up to it," he added tautly.

Tellie didn't know what he meant.

J.B. did. "Things would have ended differently if I'd known," he said in a harsh tone.

"If I'd known, too." Grange studied him. "Hell of a shame that we can't go back and do things right, isn't it?"

J.B. nodded.

"I like working at the feedlot, but it's only for a few months," he said. "If it helps, I'm no gossip. I only wanted the truth. Now I've got it." He turned to Tellie.

"I shouldn't have involved you. But I enjoyed lunch," he added quietly, and he smiled. It changed his dark eyes, made them deep and hypnotic.

"Me, too," she said, flushing a little. He really was good-looking.

Grange shrugged. "Maybe we can do it again."

She did smile then. "I'd like that."

He nodded at J.B. and left them to go to the counter and pay for his meal. J.B. sat down in the chair Grange had vacated and looked at Tellie with mingled anger and concern.

"Don't worry, J.B., he didn't spill any state secrets," she lied as she sipped tea. "He only said your father had done something to foil a romance years ago, and he wanted to know how to get in touch with the elder Mr. Hammock. He said he wanted to know for a friend of his." She hoped he believed her. She'd die if he realized she knew the whole terrible secret in his past. She felt sick at her stomach, imagining how he must feel.

He didn't answer her. He glanced at Grange as the younger man left the café, and then caught Barbara's eye and ordered coffee and apple pie.

Tellie was trying not to react at the surprise of having coffee with J.B., who'd never shared a table in a restaurant with her before. Her heart was beating double-time at just the nearness of him. She had to force herself not to stare at him with overt and visible delight.

Barbara brought coffee. He grinned at her and she grinned back. "Dating in shifts these days, huh, Tellie?" she teased.

Tellie didn't answer. She managed a faint smile, embarrassed.

J.B. sipped his coffee. He never added cream or sugar. Her eyes went to his lean, darkly tanned hands. There was a gold cat's-eye ring on his left ring finger, thick and masculine, and a thin expensive watch above it on his wrist. He was wearing a lightweight gray suit with a cream Stetson. He looked expensive and arrogant, and seductive.

"I don't like the idea of your going out with that man," J.B. told her curtly.

"It wasn't a date, J.B., it was just lunch," she said.

"It was an interrogation," he corrected. "What else did he want to know?"

She knew she'd never get away with lying. "He wanted to know about your father," she said.

"What about him?"

"If he was still alive. I told him he wasn't. That was all."

"What did he say?"

"Not much," she returned. She searched his green eyes. They were troubled and stormy. "Just that a friend had asked him to find out about your father, over some romance of yours that went bad years ago. He didn't say anything specific," she added without looking at him. He usually could tell when she was lying.

His face tautened as he looked at her. "I never meant anyone to know about what happened except Marge and me," he said tightly.

"Yes, I know, J.B.," she replied, her voice weary and

resigned. "You don't share things with outsiders."

He frowned. "You're not an outsider. You're family."

That, somehow, made things even worse. She met his eyes evenly. "You sent Jarrett out to get my graduation present. You'd never do that to Marge or the girls. And you lied about being at the graduation exercises. You were in the office with some businessman and his daughter. I gather that she was a real looker and you couldn't tear yourself away," she added with more bitterness than she realized.

His eyes almost glowed with anger. "Who told you that?"

"I took classes in ESP in college," she drawled facetiously, and with a bite in her voice. "What does it matter how I know? You lied to me!"

His indrawn breath was audible. "Damn it, Tellie!"

"Why can't you be honest with me?" she demanded. "I'm not a kid anymore. You don't have to protect me from the truth."

"You don't know the truth," he said curtly.

"Sure I do. I'm a liability you assumed because I had no family and you felt sorry for me," she replied.

"I felt sorry for you," he conceded. "But I've always included you in family activities, haven't I?"

"Oh, yes," she agreed. "I get to have Christmas and summer vacation and all the other holidays with Marge and the girls, I even get to go on overseas trips with them. I've never doubted that I was part of Marge's family," she said meaningfully.

He frowned. "Marge is part of my family."

41

"You're not part of mine, J.B.," she replied. Her heart was breaking. "I'm in the same class as your big-boobed blondes, disposable and unimportant. We don't even rate a handpicked present. You just send out the secretary to buy it, and to lie for you when you avoid events you'd rather not be forced to attend."

He glared at her. "You've got the whole thing upside down." He cursed under his breath. "Damn Grange! If he hadn't barged in . . . !"

Something was fishy here. "You know him!"

His lips made a thin line. "I know him," he admitted reluctantly. "I went to see him at the feedlot when I realized who he was. But I barely had time to say anything to him before Justin showed up. I didn't go back."

"Who is he, J.B.?" she asked, but she was sure that she already knew the answer.

"He's her brother," he said finally. "He's the brother of the woman my father kept me from marrying."

Three

The look in J.B.'s eyes was painful to Tellie, who loved him with all her heart, despite the knowledge that he was never going to be able to love her back. She could almost feel the pain that rippled through him with the words. The woman, the only woman, he'd ever loved had killed herself, because of him. It was a pain he could never escape. And now the woman's brother had shown up in his own town.

"Why is he here, do you think?" she asked.

42

J.B. sipped coffee. "Revenge, perhaps," he said tautly, "at first."

"Revenge for what?" she asked, because she knew the answer, but she didn't want him to realize how much Grange had told her.

He glanced at her appraisingly. "It's a story that doesn't concern you, Tellie," he said quietly. "It's ancient history."

She finished her own coffee. "Whatever you say, J.B.," she replied. "I have to get back to work."

She stood up. So did he. "How are you going to get back to the feedlot?" he asked abruptly. "Didn't you ride in with Grange?"

She shook her head. "It was Dutch treat."

"Are you coming to the barbecue Saturday?" he added.

It was the end of roundup, one that he gave for the ranch hands. Marge and the girls, and Tellie, were always invited. It was a comfortable routine.

Tellie had never felt less like a routine. "No, I don't think so," she said abruptly, and was pleased to see his eyelids flicker. "I have other plans."

"What other plans?" he demanded, as if he had the right to know every step she took.

She smiled carelessly. "That's not your business, J.B. See you."

She went to the counter and paid Barbara. When she left, J.B. was sitting there, brooding, his face like steel.

It wasn't until that night Tellie finally had time to digest

43

what she'd learned. She waited until the girls went to bed and then cornered Marge at the kitchen table where she was piecing a quilt.

"Do you know a family named Grange?" she asked Marge.

The older woman blinked, surprised. "Grange? Why?"

That wasn't an innocent look Marge was giving her. Tellie folded her hands on the table. "There's a man named Grange who came to work at the feedlot," she said. "He's tall and dark-eyed and dark-haired. J.B. was going to marry his sister a long time ago . . ."

"Him! Here! Dear God!" Marge exclaimed. She put her hands to her mouth. "No!"

"It's all right, Marge," she said at once. "He came looking for your father, not J.B."

Marge's eyes were wide, frightened. "You know?" she asked huskily.

She sighed heavily. "Yes. Grange told me everything. J.B. doesn't know that," she added quickly. "I said that Grange only mentioned that there was a romance gone bad in the past."

Marge drew her hands over her mouth. "It was much worse than that, Tellie. It was a nightmare," she said heavily. "I've never seen J.B. like that. He went crazy after she died. For three months, he went away and nobody even knew where he was. We couldn't find him. Dad cried . . ." She took a steadying breath. "I never understood what happened, why she did it. J.B. thought it was because they'd had an argument about her giving up her house to live with us. They parted in anger, and he didn't know what had happened until her best friend called him and gave him the news. He blamed himself. He lived with the guilt, but it ate him alive. Dad was so kind to him afterward," she added. "They'd had problems, like some fathers and sons do. They were both strong willed and domineering." She sighed. "But Dad went out of his way after that to win J.B.'s affection. I think he finally succeeded, before he had the stroke." She looked up. "Did Grange have any idea why she did such a desperate thing?"

Now things were getting sticky. Tellie hesitated. She didn't want to destroy Marge's illusions about her father. And obviously, J.B. hadn't told his sister about his father's interference that had caused the tragedy.

Marge realized that. She smiled sadly. "Tellie, my father never cared one way or the other about me. I was a girl, so I was a disappointment to him. You don't need to spare my feelings. I would like to know what Grange told you."

Tellie took a deep breath. "All right. He said that J.B.'s father came to see the girl and told her that if she married J.B., he had enough evidence to put her fourteen-year-old brother in prison for the rest of his life. The boy was involved in drugs and part of a gang."

She gasped. "So that was it! Did he tell J.B.?"

"Yes," she said. "He did. Apparently Grange only just found out himself. His father only told him when he was dying. I'm sure he was trying to spare Grange. He'll go through his own pain, realizing that he provided your father with the reason to threaten his sister."

"So many secrets," Marge said, her voice thready. "Pain and more pain. It will bring it all back, too. J.B. will relive it."

That was painful. But it wasn't all Grange's fault. "Grange just wanted to know the truth." Tellie defended the stranger. "He thought J.B. put his father up to talking to the woman."

"My brother doesn't have any problem telling people unpleasant things," she replied musingly. "He does his own dirty work."

"He does," Tellie agreed.

She frowned at the younger woman's expression. "What are you not telling me?"

She shrugged. "Jarrett let something slip."

"J.B.'s secretary? Did she? What?" she asked with a lazy smile.

"J.B. wasn't at the graduation exercises, Marge," Tellie said sadly. "He was in a meeting with a busi- nessman and his attractive daughter. He made Jarrett cover up for him. She was really upset about what he said to her. She was more upset when she found out that the present he wanted her to buy was for me, for my graduation."

"Wait a minute," Marge replied, frowning. "He lied about being at the stadium? He actually did that?"

Tellie grimaced. "Yes."

"I'll strangle him!" the older woman said forcefully.

"To what end, Marge?" Tellie asked. She felt old, tired, worn-out. "Can you make him love me? Because that isn't ever going to happen. I thought he was just a carefree playboy who liked variety in his women. But it's not that at all, is it?" She sat back in her chair, her face drawn and sad. "He blames himself because the woman he loved died. He won't risk feeling that way about another woman, setting himself up for another loss. He thinks he doesn't deserve to be happy because she killed herself."

"And all along, it was our father who did the dirty work." Marge's eyes were thoughtful. "I noticed that he seemed haunted sometimes, absolutely haunted. And I'd ask him if anything was wrong. He'd just say that people had to pay for their sins, and he hoped his punishment wouldn't be as bad as he deserved. I didn't know what he was talking about, until today. I suppose he was afraid to tell the truth, because he knew he'd lose J.B. forever."

"You couldn't have blamed him. Whatever he thought of the woman, it was J.B.'s life, and his decision. The old man couldn't live his life for him."

"You didn't know him, honey. He was just like J.B. There's the wrong way, and there's J.B.'s way. That was Dad, too."

"I see."

Marge reached across the table and held her hand. "I'm sorry you had to find it out like this. I told J.B. we should tell you, but he said—" She stopped suddenly. "Anyway, he wouldn't hear of it."

Tellie knew what Marge had avoided saying, that it was none of Tellie's business because she wasn't family. She smiled. "Don't pull your punches. I'm getting tougher by the day since I graduated."

"J.B.'s helped, hasn't he?" she said with a scowl.

"He can't change the way he feels," she said wearily. "If he was going to fall head over heels in love with me, it wouldn't have taken him seven years, Marge. Even now, I'm just a stray that he took in. Well, that *you* took in," she corrected. "J.B. decided that both of you would take care of me, but you'd do the daily work." She laughed. "And it's just like him."

"It is," Marge had to admit. She squeezed Tellie's hand and then let go. "Maybe it isn't a bad thing that you know the truth. It helps explain the way he is, and why there was never much hope for you in the first place."

"Perhaps you're right," Tellie agreed. "But you mustn't ever let J.B. know. Promise me."

"I'll never tell him what you know, Tellie," Marge agreed. She hesitated. "What is Grange like?"

"Mysterious," she replied. "Dangerous. Nobody knows much about him. They say he was in Special Forces."

"Not in the Mafia?" Marge replied dryly, and she wasn't totally kidding.

"He said that his sister's death took him right out of drug use and gang participation, although he told me at first that it was a friend and not himself," she replied. "The tragedy saved him, in fact. He felt guilty, I'm sure, when he realized that she died partially because J.B.'s father threatened to put him in prison. The awful thing

48

is that he didn't know that until three weeks ago. I expect he's hurting as much as J.B. did when he read the letter his father left him."

"That was another bad month, when J.B. got that letter attached to Dad's will," Marge said. "He got extremely drunk." She frowned. "That was the year before you graduated from high school, in fact. You came over and took a gun away from him," she added, shocked at the memory. "I yelled at you, and you wouldn't listen. You went right into his den, poured the bottle of whiskey down the sink with him yelling curses at you, and then you took away the pistol and popped the bullets out on the floor. I screamed . . ."

"You thought he'd hit me," she agreed, smiling. "But I knew better. J.B. would never hit a woman, not even if he was stinking drunk. Which he was, of course."

"You led him off to bed and stayed with him all night. The next morning he carried you into the living room where I was, and laid you out on the sofa under an Afghan. He looked very funny. When I asked him why, he said it was the first time in his life that he'd ever had a woman take care of him. Our mother wasn't domestic," she added quietly. "She was never very nurturing. She was a research chemist and her life was her work. Housekeepers raised J.B. and me. It was almost a relief for Dad, and us, when she died. I did admire her," she added. "She did a socially beneficial job. A dangerous one, too. She was working with a terrible virus strain, looking for a cure. One day in the lab, she stuck a needle, accidentally, into her hand through her

49

rubber glove and died. I was sorry, and I went to the funeral. J.B wouldn't go and neither would Dad. They said she deserted all of us for her job."

"That sounds like him," Tellie agreed.

"J.B. never stopped fussing about the way you took care of him," she recalled on a laugh. "But then he'd lose his temper when you weren't around to do it. He was furious when you spent your summer vacations with those friends at Yellowstone National Park."

"I had a good time. I miss Melody. She and I were wonderful friends, but her parents moved overseas and she had to go with them."

"I don't think I have one friend left in Jacobsville, from my school days," Marge recalled.

"What about Barbara?"

"Oh. Yes. Barbara." She chuckled. "She and that café. When we were girls, it was what she wanted most of all, to own a restaurant."

"It's a good one." Tellie hesitated. "Now, don't get angry, but she's worried about you," she added.

"Me? Why?"

"She said you had a dizzy spell."

Marge frowned. "Yes, I did. I remember. I've had two or three lately. Odd, isn't it? But then, I'm prone to migraine headaches," she added carelessly. "You get all sorts of side effects from them. In fact, I see fireworks and go blind in one eye just before I get one. The doctor calls them vascular headaches."

Tellie frowned. "Why? Does blood pressure cause them?"

Marge laughed. "Not in my case, honey. I have the lowest blood pressure in two counties. No, migraine runs in my family. My mother had them, and so did her mother."

"I'll bet J.B. doesn't have them," Tellie mused.

"That's a fact," came the laughing reply. "No, he doesn't get headaches, but he certainly gives them."

"Amen."

Marge went back to her piecing. "Maybe it's just as well that you know all about J.B. now, Tellie," she said after a minute. "Maybe it will save you any further heartache."

"Yes," the younger woman agreed sadly. "Maybe so."

Grange didn't ask her out again, but he did stop by her desk from time to time, just to see how she was. It was as if he knew how badly he'd hurt her with the information about J.B.'s past, and wanted to make amends.

"Listen," she said one day when he gave her a worried look, "I'm not stupid. I knew there was something in J.B.'s past that, well, that caused him to be the way he is. He never cared about me, except as a sort of adopted relative." She smiled. "I've got three years of college to go, you know. No place for a love life."

He studied her quietly. "Don't end up like him," he said suddenly. "Or like me. I don't think I've got it in me to trust another human being."

Her eyes were sympathetic. He was blaming himself for his sister's death. She knew it. "You'll grow old and bitter, all alone," she said.

"I'm already old and bitter," he said, and he didn't smile.

"No gray hairs," she observed.

"They're all on the inside," he shot back.

She grinned. Her whole face lit up.

He gave her an odd look and something in his expression softened, just a little.

"If you really want to look old, you should dye your hair," she pointed out.

He chuckled. "My father still had black hair when he died. He was sixty."

"Good genes," she said.

He shrugged. "Beats me. He never knew who his father was."

"Your mother?"

His face hardened. "I don't talk about her."

"Sorry."

"I didn't mean to growl," he said hesitantly. "I'm not used to women."

"Imagine a man ever admitting that!" she exclaimed with mock surprise.

He cocked an eyebrow. "You're sassy."

"Yes, I am. Nice of you to notice. Now would you mind leaving? Justin's going to come back any minute. He won't like having you flirt with me on his time."

"I don't flirt," he shot back.

"Well, excuse me!"

He shifted. "Maybe I flirt a little. It isn't intentional."

"God forbid! Who'd want to marry you?" she asked curiously.

He scowled. "Look here, I'm not a bad person."

"Well, I wouldn't want to marry you," she persisted.

"Who asked you?" he asked curtly.

"Not you, for sure," she returned. "And don't bother," she added when he started to speak. "I'm such a rare catch that I have men salivating in the yard, wherever I go."

His dark eyes started to twinkle. "Why?"

"Because I can make French pastry," she told him. "With real whipped cream and custard fillings."

He pursed his lips. "Well!"

"See? I'm quite a catch. Too bad you're not in the running."

He frowned. "Even if I were interested, what would I do with a wife?"

"You don't know?" She gave him such an expression of shock and horror that he burst out laughing.

She grinned at him. "See there? You're improving all the time. I'm a good influence, I am!"

"You're a pain in the neck," he returned. "But not bad company." He shrugged. "Like movies?"

"What sort?"

"Science fiction?"

She chuckled. "You bet."

"I'll check and see what's playing at the theater Saturday, if you're game."

Saturday was the barbecue at J.B.'s that she was determined not to attend. Here was her excuse to miss it. She liked Grange. Besides, no way was she going to sit home and eat her heart out over J.B., especially when she'd already told him that she had other plans. "I'm game."

"Your adopted family won't like it," he said slowly.

"Marge won't mind," she said, certain that it was true. "And I don't care what J.B. thinks."

He nodded. "Okay. It's a date. We'll work out the details Friday."

"Fine. Now please go away," she added, glancing at the door, where Justin was just coming inside the building. "Or we may both be out looking for work on Monday!"

He grinned and left her before Justin got the door closed.

Marge was less enthusiastic than Tellie had expected. In fact, she seemed disturbed.

"Does the phrase, rubbing salt on an open wound, ring any chimes?" Marge asked her somberly.

"But Grange didn't do anything," she protested. "He was as much a victim as J.B. was."

Marge hesitated, uneasy. "I understand that. But he's connected with it. J.B. will see it as a personal attack on him, by both of you."

"That's absurd!"

"It isn't, if you remember the way my brother is."

For the first time since Grange had asked her out, Tellie wasn't sure she was doing the right thing. She didn't want to hurt J.B., even if he'd given her reason. On the other hand, it was a test of control, his over hers. If she gave in now, she'd be giving in forever. Marge was her friend, but J.B. was Marge's brother. It was a tangled situation.

Marge put an arm around her. "Don't worry yourself to death, honey," she said gently. "If you really want to go out with him, go ahead. I'm just saying that J.B. is going to take it personally. But you can't let him run your life."

Tellie hugged her back. "Thanks, Marge."

"Why don't you want to go to the barbecue?" the older woman asked.

Tellie grimaced. "Miss runner-up beauty queen will be there, won't she?"

Marge pursed her lips. "So that's it."

"Don't you dare tell him," came the terse reply.

"Never." Marge sighed. "I didn't even think about that. No wonder you're so anxious to stay away."

"She's really gorgeous, isn't she?"

Marge looked old and wise. "She's just like all the other ones before her, Tellie, tall and blond and stacked. Not much in the way of intelligence. You know," she added thoughtfully, "I don't think J.B. really likes intelligent women much."

"Maybe he feels threatened by us."

"Don't you believe it," Marge scoffed. "He's got a business degree from Yale, you know."

"I'd forgotten."

"No, I think it has to do with our mother," she continued. "She was always running down our father, making him feel like an idiot. She was forever going to conventions with one of her research partners. Later, they had a serious affair. That was just before she died."

"J.B. didn't have a great respect for women, I guess."

"Not in his younger days. Then he got engaged, and tragedy followed." She seemed far away. "I lost my first love to another woman, and then my husband died of an embolism after surgery." She shook her head. "J.B. and I have poor track records with happily ever after."

Tellie felt sad for both of them. "I suppose it would make you gun-shy, when it came to love."

"Love?" Marge laughed. "J.B. doesn't believe in it anymore." She gave Tellie a sad, gentle appraisal. "But you should. Maybe Grange will be the best thing that ever happened to you. It wouldn't hurt to show J.B. that you're not dying of a broken heart, either."

"He won't notice," Tellie said with conviction. "He used to complain that I was always underfoot."

"Not recently."

"I've been away at college for four years more or less," she reminded the older woman. That reminded her of graduation, which he hadn't attended. It still stung.

"And going away for three more." Marge smiled. "Live your life, Tellie. You don't have to answer to any-body. Be happy."

"That's easier said than done," Tellie pointed out. She smiled at Marge. "Okay. If you don't mind me dating Grange, J.B. can think what he likes. I don't care."

Which wasn't the truth, exactly.

Grange was good company when he relaxed and

forgot that Tellie was a friend of J.B.'s.

The movie was unforgettable, a film about a misfit crew aboard a space-going freighter who were protecting a girl from some nasty authorities. It was funny and sweet, and full of action.

They came out of the theater smiling.

"It's been a good year for science-fiction movies," he remarked.

"It has," Tellie agreed, "but that was the best I've seen so far. I missed the series when it was on television. I guess I'll have to buy the DVD set."

He gave her an amused look. "You're nice to take around," he said on the way to his big gray truck. "If I weren't a confirmed bachelor, you'd be at the top of my list of prospects."

"Why, what a nice thing to say!" she exclaimed. "Do you mind if I quote you frequently?"

He gave her a quick look and relaxed a little when she laughed. "Quote me?" he asked quizzically.

Her shoulders rose and fell. "It's just that nobody ever said I was marriageable before, you see," she told him. "I figure with an endorsement like that, the sky's the limit. I mean, I won't be in college forever. A woman has to think about the future."

Grange stared at her in the light from the parking lot. "I don't think I've ever been around anyone like you. Most women these days are too aggressive for my taste."

Her eyebrows arched. "Like doormats, do we?" she teased.

He shook his head. "It's not that. I like a woman with spirit. But I don't like being seen as a party favor."

"Now you know how women feel," she pointed out.

"I never treated a woman that way," he returned.

"A lot of men have."

"I suppose so," he conceded. He gave her a smile. "I enjoyed tonight."

"Me, too."

"We'll do it again sometime."

She smiled back. "Suits me."

Grange dropped her off at Marge's house, but he didn't try to kiss her good-night. He was a gentleman in the best sense of the word. Tellie liked him. But her heart still ached for J.B.

Tellie assumed that Marge and the girls were in bed, because the lights were all off inside. She locked the door behind her and started toward the staircase when a light snapped on in the living room.

She whirled, surprised, and looked right into J. B. Hammock's seething green eyes.

Four

"What . . . are you doing here?" she blurted out, flushing at the way he was looking at her. "Has something happened to Marge or the girls?" she added at once, uneasy.

"No. They're fine."

She moved into the room, putting her purse and coat

on a chair, her slender body in jeans with pink embroidered roses and a pink tank top that matched. Her pale eyes searched his dark green ones curiously. She ran a nervous hand through her wavy dark hair and grimaced. He looked like an approaching storm.

"Then why are you here?" she asked when the silence became oppressive.

His eyes slid over her body in the tight jeans and tank top and narrowed with reluctant appreciation. He was also in jeans, but his were without decoration. A chambray shirt covered his broad, muscular chest and long arms. It was unfastened at the throat. He usually dressed casually for barbecues, and this one didn't seem to be an exception.

"You went to a movie with Grange," he said.

"Yes."

His face tautened. "I don't like you going out with him."

Her thin dark eyebrows arched. "I'm almost twenty-two, J.B."

"Jacobsville is full of eligible bachelors."

"Yes, I know. Grange is one of them."

"Damn it, Tellie!"

She drew in a steadying breath. It was hard not to give in to J.B. She'd spent most of her adolescence doing exactly that. But this was a test of her newfound independence. She couldn't let him walk all over her. Despite his reasons for not wanting her around Grange, she couldn't let him dictate her future. Particularly since he wasn't going to be part of it.

"I'm not marrying him, J.B.," she said quietly. "He's just someone to go out with."

His lean jaw tautened. "He's part of a painful episode in my past," he said flatly. "It's disloyal of you to take his side against me. I'm not pushing the point, but I gave you a home when you needed one."

Her eyes narrowed. "*You* gave me a home? No, J.B., *you* didn't give me a home. You decided that *Marge* would give me a home," she said emphatically.

"Same thing," he bit off.

"It isn't," she replied. "You don't put yourself out for anybody. You make gestures, but somebody else has to do the dirty work."

"That's not how it was, and you know it," he said curtly. "You were fourteen years old. How would it have looked, to have you living with me? Especially with my lifestyle."

She wanted to argue that, but she couldn't. "I suppose you have a point."

He didn't reply. He just watched her.

She moved to the sofa and perched on one of its broad, floral-patterned arms. "I'm very grateful for what your family has done for me," she said gently. "But nobody can say that I haven't pulled my weight. I've cleaned and cooked for Marge and the girls, been a live-in baby-sitter, helped keep her books—I haven't just parked myself here and taken advantage of the situation."

"I never said you did," he replied.

"You're implying it," she shot back. "I can't remember

when I've ever dated anybody around here . . . !"

"Of course not, you were too busy mooning over me!"

Her face went white. Then it slowly blossomed into red rage. She stood up, eyes blazing. "Yes," she said. "I was, wasn't I? Mooning over you while you indulged yourself with starlet after debutante after Miss Beauty Contest winner! Oh, excuse me, Miss Runner-up Beauty Contest winner," she drawled insolently.

He glared at her. "My love life is none of your business."

"Don't be absurd," she retorted. "It's everybody's business. You were in a tabloid story just last week, something about you and the living fashion doll being involved in some sleazy love triangle in Hollywood . . ."

"Lies," he shot back, "and I'm suing!"

"Good luck," she said. "My point is, I date a nice man who hasn't hurt anybody . . ."

He let out a vicious curse, interrupting her, and moved closer, towering over her. "He was Special Forces in Iraq," he told her coldly, "and he was brought up on charges for excessive force during an incursion! He actually slugged his commanding officer and stuffed him in the trunk of a civilian car!"

Her eyes widened. "Did he, really?" she mused, fascinated.

"It isn't funny," he snapped. "The man is a walking time bomb, waiting for the spark to set him off. I don't want him around you when it happens. He was forced out of the army, Tellie, he didn't go willingly! He had the choice of a court-martial or an honorable discharge."

She wondered how he knew so much about the other man, but she didn't pursue it. "It was an honorable discharge, then?" she emphasized.

He took off his white Stetson and ran an irritated hand through his black hair. "I can't make you see it, can I? The man's dangerous."

"He's in good company in Jacobsville, then, isn't he?" she replied. "I mean, we're like a resort for ex-mercs and ex-military, not to mention the number of ex-federal law enforcement people . . ."

"Grange has enemies," he interrupted.

"So do you, J.B.," she pointed out. "Remember that guy who broke into your house with a .45 automatic and tried to shoot you over a horse deal?"

"He was a lunatic."

"If the bullet hadn't been a dud, you'd be dead," she reminded him.

"Ancient history," he said. "You're avoiding the subject."

"I am not likely to be shot by one of Grange's mythical old enemies while watching a science-fiction film at the local theater!" Her small hands balled at her hips. "The only thing you're mad about is that you can't make me do what you want me to do anymore," she challenged.

A deep, dark sensuality came into his green eyes and one corner of his chiseled mouth turned up. "Can't I, now?" he drawled, moving forward.

She backed up. "Oh, no, you don't," she warded him off. "Go home and thrill your beauty queen, J.B., I'm not on the market."

He lifted an eyebrow at her flush and the faint rustle of her heartbeat against her tank top. "Aren't you?"

She backed up one more step, just in case. "What happened to you was . . . was tragic, but it was a long time ago, J.B., and Grange wasn't responsible for it," she argued. "He was surely as much a victim as you were, especially when he found out the truth. Can't you imagine how he must have felt, when he knew that his own actions cost him his sister's life?"

He seemed to tauten all over. "He told you all of it?"

She hadn't meant to let that slip. He made her nervous when he came close like this. She couldn't think. "You'd never have told me. Neither would Marge. Okay, it's not my business," she added when he looked threatening, "but I can have an opinion."

"Grange was responsible," he returned coldly. "His own delinquency made it impossible for her to get past my father."

"That's not true," Tellie said, her voice quiet and firm. "If I wanted to marry someone, and his father tried to blackmail me, I'd have gone like a shot to the man and told him . . . !"

The effect the remark had on him was scary. He seemed to grow taller, and his eyes were terrible. His deep, harsh voice interrupted her. "Stop it."

She did. She didn't have the maturity, or the confidence, to argue the point with him. But she wouldn't have killed herself, she was sure of it. She'd have embarrassed J.B.'s father, shamed him, defied him. She wasn't the sort of person to take blackmail lying down.

"You don't know what you're talking about," he said, his eyes furious. "You'd never sacrifice another human being's life or freedom to save yourself."

"Maybe not," she conceded. "But I wouldn't kill myself, either." She was going to add that it was a cowardly thing to do, but the way J.B. was looking at her kept her quiet.

"She loved me. She was going to have to give me up, and she couldn't bear to go on living that way. In her own mind, she didn't have a choice," he said harshly. He searched her quiet face. "You can't comprehend an emotion that powerful, can you, Tellie? After all, what the hell would you know about love? You're still wrapped up in dreams of happily ever after, cotton-candy kisses and hand-holding! You don't know what it is to want someone so badly that it's physically painful to be separated from them. You don't understand the violence of desire." He laughed coldly. "Maybe that's just as well. You couldn't handle an affair!"

"Good, because I don't want one!" she replied angrily. He made her feel small, inadequate. It hurt. "I'm not going to pass myself around like a cigarette to any man who wants me, just to prove how liberated I am! And when I marry, I won't want some oversexed libertine who jumps into bed with any woman who wants him!"

He went very still and quiet. His face was like a

64

drawn cord, his eyes green flames as he glared down at her.

"Sorry," she said uneasily. "That didn't come out the way I meant it. I just don't think that a man, or a woman, who lives that permissively can ever settle down and be faithful. I want a stable marriage that children will fit into, not an endless round of new partners."

"Children," he scoffed.

"Yes, children." Her eyes softened as she thought of them. "A whole house full of them, one day, when I'm through school."

"With Grange as their father?"

She gaped at him. "I just went to a movie with him, J.B.!"

"If you get involved with him, I'll never forgive you," he said in a voice as cold as the grave.

"Well, golly gee whiz, that would be a tragedy, wouldn't it? Just think, I'd never get another present that you sent Jarrett to buy for me!"

His breath was coming quickly through his nose. His lips were flattened. He didn't have a comeback. That seemed to make him angrier. He took another step toward her.

She backed up a step. "You should be happy to have me out of your life," she pointed out uneasily. "I was never more than an afterthought anyway, J.B. Just a pest. All I did was get in your way."

He stopped just in front of her. He looked oddly frustrated. "You're still getting in my way," he said enigmatically. "I know that no matter what Marge may have said, she and the girls were disappointed that you missed the barbecue. It's the first time in seven years that you've done that, and for a man who represents as much hurt to Marge herself as he does to me."

She frowned. "But why? She never knew Grange!"

"You told her what my father did," he said deliberately.

She grimaced. "I didn't mean to!" she confessed. "I didn't want to. But she said it wouldn't matter."

"And you don't know her any better than that, after so long in her house? She was devastated."

She felt worse than ever. "I guess it was rough on you, too, when you found out what he'd done," she said unexpectedly.

His expression was odd. Reserved. Uneasy. "I've never hated a human being so much in all my life," he said huskily. "And he was dead. There was nothing I could do to him, no way I could pay him back for ruining my life and taking hers. You can't imagine how I felt."

"I'm sure he was sorry about it," she said, having gleaned that from what Marge had said about the way he'd treated J.B. "You know he'd have taken it back if he could have. He must have loved you, very much. Marge said that he would have been afraid of losing you if he'd told the truth. You were his only son."

"Forgiveness comes hard to me," he said.

She knew that. He'd never held any grudges against her, but she knew people in town who'd crossed him years ago, and he still went out of his way to snub them.

He didn't forgive, and he never forgot.

"Are you so perfect that you never make mistakes?" she wondered out loud.

"None to date," he replied, and he didn't smile.

"Your day is coming."

His eyes narrowed as he stared down at her. "You won't leave Grange alone. Is that final?"

She swallowed. "Yes. It's final."

He gave her a look as cold as death. His head jerked. "Your choice."

He turned on his heel and stalked out of the room. She watched him go with nervous curiosity. What in the world did he mean?

Marge was very quiet at breakfast the next day. Dawn and Brandi kept giving Tellie odd looks, too. They went off to church with friends. Marge wasn't feeling well, so she stayed home and Tellie stayed with her. Something was going on. She wondered what it was.

"Is there something I've done that I need to apologize for?" she asked Marge while they were making lunch in the kitchen.

Marge drew in a slow breath. "No, of course not," she denied gently. "It's just J.B., wanting his own way and making everybody miserable because he can't get it."

"If you want me to stop dating Grange, just say so," Tellie told her. "I won't do it for J.B., but I will do it for you."

Marge smiled at her gently. She reached over and

patted Tellie's hand. "You don't have to make any such sacrifices. Let J.B. stew."

"Maybe the man does bring back some terrible memories," she murmured. "J.B. looked upset when he talked about it. He must . . . he must have loved her very much."

"He was twenty-one," Marge recalled. "Love is more intense at that age, I think. Certainly it was for me. She was J.B.'s first real affair. He wasn't himself the whole time he knew her. I thought she was too old for him, too, but he wouldn't hear a word we said about her. He turned against me, against Dad, against the whole world. He ran off to get married and said he'd never come back. But she argued with him. We never knew exactly why, but when she took her own life, he blamed himself. And then when he learned the truth . . . well, he was never the same."

"I'm sorry it was like that for him," she said, understanding how he would have felt. She felt like that about J.B. At least, she thought, she wasn't losing him to death—just to legions of other women.

Marge put down the spoon she was using to stir beef stew and turned to Tellie. "I would have told you about her, eventually, even if Grange hadn't shown up," she said quietly. "I knew it would hurt, to know he felt like that about another woman. But at least you'd understand why you couldn't get close to him. You can't fight a ghost, Tellie. She's perfect in his mind, like a living, breathing photograph that never ages, never has faults, never creates problems. No living woman will ever top her in J.B.'s mind. Loving him, while he feels like that about a ghost, would kill your very soul."

"Yes, I understand that now," Tellie said heavily. She stared out the window, seeing nothing. "How little we really know people."

"You can live with someone for years and not know them," Marge agreed. "I just don't want you to waste your life on my brother. You deserve better."

Tellie winced, but she didn't let Marge see. "I'll get married one of these days and have six kids."

"You will," Marge agreed, smiling gently. "And I'll spoil your kids the way you've spoiled mine."

"The girls didn't look too happy this morning," Tellie remarked.

Marge grimaced. "J.B. had them in the kitchen helping prepare canapés," she said. "They didn't even get to dance."

"But, why?"

"They're just kids," Marge said ruefully. "They aren't old enough to notice eligible bachelors. To hear J.B. tell it, at least."

"But that's outrageous! They're sixteen and seventeen years old. They're not kids!"

"To J.B., you all are, Tellie."

She glowered. "Maybe Brandi and Dawn would like to go halves with me on a really mean singing telegram."

"J.B. would slug the singer, and we'd get sued," Marge said blithely. "Let it go, honey. I know things look dark at the moment, but they'll get better. We have to look to the future."

"I guess."

"The girls should be home any minute. I'll start dishing up while you set the table."

Tellie went to do it, her heart around her ankles.

If she'd wondered what J.B. meant with his cryptic remark, it became crystal clear in the days that followed. He came to the house to see Marge and pretended that Tellie wasn't there. If he passed her on the street at lunchtime, he didn't see her. For all intents and purposes, she had become the invisible woman. He was paying her back for dating Grange.

Which made her more determined, of course, to go out with the man. She didn't care if J.B. snubbed her forever; he wasn't dictating her life!

Grange discovered J.B.'s new attitude the following Saturday, when he took Tellie to a local community theater presentation of *Arsenic and Old Lace*. J.B. came in with his gorgeous blonde and sat down in the row across from Tellie and Grange. He didn't look their way all night, and when he passed them on the way out, he didn't speak.

"What the hell is wrong with him?" Grange asked her on the way home.

"He's paying me back for dating you," she said simply.

"That's low."

"That's J.B.," she replied.

"Do you want me to stop asking you out, Tellie?" he asked quietly.

"I do not. J.B. isn't telling me what to do," she replied. "He can ignore me all he likes. I'll ignore him back."

Grange was quiet. "I shouldn't have come here."

"You just wanted to know what happened," she defended him. "Nobody could blame you for that. She was your sister."

He pulled up in front of Marge's house and cut off the engine. "Yes, she was. She and Dad were the only family I had, but I was rotten to them. I ran wild when I hit thirteen. I got in with a bad crowd, joined a gang, used drugs—you name it, I did it. I still don't understand why I didn't end up in jail."

"Her death saved you, didn't it?" she asked.

He nodded, his face averted. "I didn't admit it at the time, though. She was such a sweet woman. She always thought of other people before she thought of herself. She was all heart. It must have been a walk in the park for Hammock's father to convince her that she was ruining J.B.'s life."

"Can you imagine how the old man felt," she began slowly, "because he was always afraid that J.B. would find out the truth and know what he'd done. He had to know that he'd have lost J.B.'s respect, maybe even his love, and he had to live with that until he died. I don't imagine he was a very happy person, even if he did what he felt was the right thing."

"He didn't even know my sister, my dad said," Grange replied. "He wouldn't talk to her. He was sure she was a gold digger, just after J.B.'s money."

"How horrible, to think like that," she murmured thoughtfully. "I guess I wouldn't want to be rich. You'd never be sure if people liked you for what you were or what you had."

"The old man seemed to have an overworked sense of his own worth."

"It sounds like it, from what Marge says."

"Did you ever know him?"

"Only by reputation," she replied. "He was in the nursing home when I came to live with Marge."

"What is she like?"

She smiled. "The exact opposite of J.B. She's sweet and kind, and she never knows a stranger. She isn't suspicious or crafty, and she never hurts people deliberately."

"But her brother does?"

"J.B. never pulls his punches," she replied. "I suppose you know where you stand with him. But he's uncomfortable to be around sometimes, when he's in a bad mood."

He studied her curiously. "How long have you been in love with him?"

She laughed nervously. "I don't love J.B.! I hate him!"

"How long," he persisted, softening the question with a smile.

She shrugged. "Since I was fourteen, I suppose. I hero-worshiped him at first, followed him everywhere, baked him cookies, waylaid him when he went riding and tagged along. He was amazingly tolerant, when I was younger. Then I graduated from high school and we became enemies. He likes to rub it in that I'm vulnerable when he's around. I don't understand why."

"Maybe he doesn't understand why, either," he ventured.

"You think?" She smiled across the seat at him. "I'm surprised that J.B. hasn't tried to run you out of town."

"He has."

"What?"

He smiled faintly. "He went to see Justin Ballenger yesterday."

"About you?" she wondered.

He nodded. "He said that I was a bad influence on you, and he wondered if I wouldn't be happier working somewhere else."

"What did Justin say?" she asked.

He chuckled. "That he could run his own feedlot without Hammock's help, and that he wasn't firing a good worker because of Hammock's personal issues."

"Well!"

"I understand that Hammock is pulling his cattle out of the feedlot and having them trucked to Kansas, to a feedlot there for finishing."

"But that's horrible!" Tellie exclaimed.

"Justin said something similar, with a few more curse words attached," Grange replied. "I felt bad to cause such problems for him, but he only laughed. He said Hammock would lose money on the deal, and he didn't care. He wasn't being ordered around by a man ten years his junior."

"That sounds like Justin," she agreed, smiling. "Good for him."

He shrugged. "It doesn't solve the problem, though," he told her. "It's only the first salvo. Hammock won't quit. He wants me out of your life, whatever it takes."

"No, it's not about me," she said sadly. "He doesn't like being reminded of what he lost. Marge said so."

Grange's dark eyes studied her quietly. "He didn't want you to know about my sister," he said after a minute. "I ticked him off that first day we went to lunch, by telling you the family secret."

"Marge said that she would have told me herself eventually."

"Why?"

She smiled. "She thinks I'd wear my heart out on J.B., and she's right. I would have. He'll never get past his lovely ghost to any sort of relationship with a real woman. I'm not going to waste my life aching for a man I can't have."

"That's sensible," he agreed. "But he's been part of your life for a long time. He's become a habit."

She nodded, her eyes downcast. "That's just what he is. A habit."

He drew in a long breath. "If you want to stop seeing me . . ."

"I do not," she said at once. "I really enjoy going out with you, Grange."

He smiled, because it was obvious that she meant it. "I like your company, too." He hesitated. "Just friends," he added slowly.

She smiled back. "Just friends."

His eyes were distant. "I'm at a turning point in my life," he confessed. "I'm not sure where I'm headed. But I know I'm not ready for anything serious."

"Neither am I." She leaned her head against the back of the seat and studied him. "Do you think you might stay here, in Jacobsville?"

"I don't know. I've got some problems to work out."

"Join the club," she said, and grinned at him.

He laughed. "I like the way I feel with you. J.B. can go hang. We'll present a united front."

"Just as long as J.B. doesn't go and hang us!" she exclaimed.

Five

Grange liked to bowl. Tellie had never tried the sport, but he taught her. She persuaded Marge to let the girls come with them one night. Marge tagged along, but she didn't bowl. She sat at the table sipping coffee and watching her brood fling the big balls down the alley.

"It's fun!" Tellie laughed. She'd left the field to the three experts who were making her look sick with her less-than-perfect bowling.

"That's why you're sitting here with me, is it?" Marge teased.

She shrugged. "I'm a lemon," she confessed. "Nothing I do ever looks good."

"That's not true," Marge disputed. "You cook like an angel and you're great in history. You always make A's."

"Two successes out of a hundred false starts," Tellie sighed.

"You're just depressed because J.B.'s ignoring you," Marge said, cutting to the heart of the matter.

"Guilty," Tellie had to admit. "Maybe I should have listened."

"Bull. If you give J.B. the upper hand, he'll walk all over you. The way you used to be, when you were fourteen, I despaired of what would happen if he ever really noticed you. He'd have destroyed your life, Tellie. You'd have become his doormat. He'd have hated that as much as you would."

"Think so? He seems pretty uncomfortable with me when I stand up to him."

"But he respects you for it."

Tellie propped her elbows on the table and rested her chin in her hands. "Does the beauty queen runner-up stand up to him?" she wondered.

"Are you kidding? She won't go to the bathroom without asking J.B. if he thinks it's a good idea!" came the dry response. "She's not giving up all those perks. He gave her a diamond dinner ring last week for her birthday."

That hurt. "I suppose he picked it out himself?"

Marge sighed. "I think she did."

"I can't believe I've wasted four years of my life mooning over that man," Tellie said, wondering aloud at her own stupidity. "I turned down dates with really nice men in college because I was hung up on J.B. Well, never again."

"What sort of nice men?" Marge queried, trying to change the subject.

Tellie grinned. "One was an anthropology major, working on his Ph.D. He's going to devote his life to a dig in Montana, looking for PaleoIndian sites."

"Just imagine, Tellie, you could work beside him with a toothbrush . . ."

"Stop that," Tellie chuckled. "I don't think I'm cut out for dust and dirt and bones."

"What other nice men?"

"There was a friend of one of my professors," she recalled. "He raises purebred Appaloosa stallions when he isn't hunting for meteorites all over the world. He was a character!"

"Why would you hunt meteorites?" Marge wondered.

"Well, he sold one for over a hundred thousand dollars to a collector," the younger woman replied, tongue in cheek.

Marge whistled. "Wow! Maybe I'll get a metal detector and go out searching for them myself!"

That was a real joke, because Marge had inherited half of her father's estate. She lived in a simple house and she never lived high. But she could have, if she'd wanted to. She felt that the girls shouldn't have too much luxury in their formative years. Maybe she was right. Certainly, Brandi and Dawn had turned out very well. They were responsible and kindhearted, and they never felt apart from fellow students.

Tellie glanced at the lanes, where Grange was throwing a ball down the aisle with force, and grace. He had a rodeo rider's physique, lean in the hips and wide in the shoulders. Odd, the way he moved, Tellie mused, like a hunter.

"He really is a dish," she murmured, deep in thought.

Marge nodded. "He is unusual," she said. "Imagine a boy on a path that deadly turning his life around."

"J.B. said he was forced out of the military."

Marge gaped at her. "He told you that? How did he know?"

Tellie glowered. "I expect he's had a firm of private detectives on overtime, finding out everything they could about him. J.B. loves to have leverage if he has to go against people."

"He won't bother Grange," Marge said. "He just wants to make sure that the man isn't a threat to you."

"He wants to decide who I marry, and how many kids I have," she returned coolly. "But he's not going to."

"That's the spirit, Tellie," Marge chuckled.

"All the same," Tellie replied, "I wish he wouldn't snub me. I'm beginning to feel like a ghost."

"He'll get over it."

"You think so? I wonder."

Saturday came, and Grange had something to do for Justin, so Tellie stayed home and helped Marge clean house.

A car drove up out front and two car doors slammed. Tellie was on her hands and knees in the kitchen, scrubbing the tile with a brush while Marge cleaned upstairs. J.B. walked in with a ravishing young blond woman on his arm. She was tall and beautifully made, with a model-perfect face and teeth, and hair to her waist in back.

"I thought they abolished indentured servitude," J.B. drawled, looking pointedly at Tellie.

She looked up at him with cold eyes, pushing sweaty hair out of her eyes with the back of a dirty hand. "It's called housecleaning, J.B. I'm sure you have no idea what it consists of."

"Nell takes care of all that," he said. "This is Bella Dean," he introduced the blonde, wrapping a long arm around her and smiling at her warmly.

"Nice to meet you," Tellie said, forcing a smile. "I'd shake hands, but I'm sure you'd rather not." She indicated her dirty hands.

Bella didn't answer her. She beamed up at J.B. "Didn't we come to take your sister and your nieces out to eat?" she asked brightly. "I'm sure the kitchen help doesn't need an audience."

Tellie got to her feet, slammed the brush down on the floor and walked right up to the blonde, who actually backed away.

"What would you know about honest work, lady, unless you call lying on your back, work . . . !"

"Tellie!" J.B. bit off.

The blonde gasped. "Well, I never!"

"I'll bet there's not much you've never," Tellie said coldly. "For your information, I don't work here. Marge gave me a home when my mother died, and I earn my keep. When I'm not scrubbing floors, I go to college to earn a degree, so that I can make a living for myself," she added pointedly. "I'm sure you won't ever have a similar problem, as long as your looks last."

"Tellie!" J.B. repeated.

"I'd rather be pretty than smart," the blonde said carelessly. "Who'd want to give you diamonds?" she scoffed.

Tellie balled a fist.

"Go tell Marge we're here," he demanded, his eyes making cold threats.

"Tell her yourself, J.B.," Tellie replied, eyes flashing. "I'm not anybody's servant."

She turned and left the room, so furious that she was shaking all over.

J.B. followed her right into her bedroom and closed the door behind them.

"What the hell was that all about?" he asked furiously.

"I am not going to be looked down on by any smarmy blond tart!" she exclaimed.

"You behaved like a child!" he returned.

"She started it," she reminded him.

"She thought you were the housekeeper," he replied. "She didn't know you from a button."

"She'll know me next time, won't she?"

He moved closer, glaring at her. "You're so jealous you're vibrating with it," he accused, his green eyes narrowing. "You want me."

She drew in a sharp breath and her hands tightened into fists. "I do not," she retorted.

He moved a step closer, so that he was right up against her. His big hand went to her cheek, smoothing over it. His thumb rubbed maddeningly at her lower lip. "You want me," he whispered deeply, bending. "I can feel your heart beating. You ache for me to touch you."

"J.B., if . . . if you don't . . . stop," she faltered, fighting his arrogance and her own weakness.

"You don't want me to stop, baby," he murmured, his chiseled mouth poised just over her parted lips. "That's the last thing you want." His thumb tugged her lower lip down and he nibbled softly at the upper one. He heard her breath catch, felt her body shiver. His eyes began to glitter with something like triumph. "I can feel your heart beating. You're waking up. I could do any-thing I liked to you, whenever I pleased, and we both know it, Tellie."

A husky little moan escaped her tight throat and she moved involuntarily, her body brushing against his, her mouth lifting, pleading, her hands going to his hard upper arms to hold him there. She hated him for doing this to her, but she couldn't resist him.

He knew it. He laughed. He pulled away from her, arrogance in his whole bearing. He smiled, and it wasn't a nice smile at all. "She likes to kiss me, too, Tellie," he said deliberately. "But she's no prude. She likes to take her clothes off, and I don't even have to coax her . . ."

She slapped him. She was humiliated, hurt, furious. She put the whole weight of her arm behind it, sobbing.

He didn't even react, except to lift an eyebrow and

smile even more arrogantly. "Next time I bring her over to see Marge, you'd better be more polite, Tellie," he warned softly, and the deep edge of anger glittered in his green eyes. "Or I'll do this in front of her."

Tellie was horrified at even the thought. Her face went pale. Tears brightened her eyes, but she would have died rather than shed them. "There aren't enough bad words in the English language to describe what you are, J.B.," she said brokenly.

"Oh, you'll think of some eventually, I'm sure. And if you can't, you can always give me another one of those god-awful dragon ties, can't you?"

"I bought boxes of them!" she slung at him.

He only laughed. He gave her a last probing look and went out of the room, leaving the door open behind him.

"Where have you been?" the blonde demanded in a honeyed tone.

"Just having a little overdue discussion. We'd better go. See you, Marge."

There were muffled voices. A door closed. Two car doors slammed. An engine roared.

Marge knocked gently and came into Tellie's room, her whole look apprehensive. She grimaced.

Tellie was as white as a sheet, shaking with rage and humiliation.

"I'll tell him not to bring her here again," Marge said firmly. She put her arms around Tellie and gathered her close. "It's all right."

"He's the devil in a suit," Tellie whispered huskily. "The very devil, Marge. I never, never want to see him again."

The thin arms closed around her and rocked her while she cried. Marge wondered why J.B. had to be so cruel to a woman who loved him this much. She had a good idea of what he'd done. It was unfair of him. He didn't want Tellie. Why couldn't he leave her alone? He'd brought his latest lover here deliberately. Tellie had refused to go to the barbecue, avoiding being around the woman, so J.B. had brought her over to Marge's to rub it in. He wanted Tellie to see how beautiful the woman was, how devoted she was to J.B. He was angry that he couldn't stop her from seeing Grange, not even by snubbing her. This was low, even for J.B.

"I don't know what's gotten into my brother," Marge said aloud. "But I'm very sorry, Tellie."

"It's not your fault. We don't get to choose our relatives, more's the pity."

"I wouldn't choose J.B. for a brother, after today." She drew away, her dark eyes twinkling, mischievous. "Tellie, the girls wouldn't let J.B. introduce them to his girlfriend. They gave her vicious looks, glared at J.B. and went to Dawn's room and locked themselves in. He's mad at them now, too."

"Good. Maybe he'll stay at his own house."

"I wouldn't bet on that," Marge thought, but she didn't say it aloud. Tellie had stood enough for one day.

Grange took Tellie with him around the feedlot the next

week, explaining how they monitored statistics and mixed the feed for the various lots of cattle. He'd asked Justin for permission. The older man was glad to give it. He liked the strange young man who'd come to work for him. It was a compliment, because Justin didn't like many people at all.

Grange propped one big, booted foot on the bottom rail of one of the enclosures, with his arms folded on the top one. His dark eyes had a faraway look. "This is good country," he said. "I grew up in West Texas. Mostly we've got desert and cactus and mountains over around El Paso. This is green heaven."

"Yes, it is. I love it here," she confessed. "I go to school in Houston. It's green there, too, but the trees are nestled in concrete."

He chuckled. "Do you like college?"

"I do."

"I went myself, in the army."

"What did you study?"

He grinned at her. "Besides weapons and tactics, you mean?" He chuckled. "I studied political science."

She was surprised, and showed it. "That was your major?"

"Part of it. I did a double major, in political science and Arab dialects."

"You mean, you can speak Arabic?"

He nodded. "Farsi, Bedouin, several regional dialects. Well, and the Romance languages."

"All three of them?" she asked, surprised.

"All three." He glanced at her and smiled at her

84

expression. "Languages will get you far in government service and the military. I mustered out as a major."

She tried not to let on that she'd heard about his release from the service. "Did you like the military?" she asked with deliberate carelessness.

He gave her a slow appraisal from dark, narrowed eyes. "Gossip travels fast in small towns, doesn't it?" he wondered aloud. "I expect Hammock had something to do with it."

She sighed. "Probably did," she had to admit. "He did everything he could to keep me from going out with you."

"So he holds grudges," he remarked. "Lucky for him that I don't, or he'd be sleeping with guards at every door and a gun under his pillow. If it hadn't been for him, I'd still have my sister."

"Maybe he thinks that, except for you, and his father, he'd be happily married with kids now."

He shrugged. "Nobody came out of it laughing," he said. He looked down at her, puzzled. "If he wanted you to stop going out with me, why haven't you?"

She smiled sadly. "I got tired of being a carpet," she said.

He cocked his head. "Walked all over you, did he?"

She nodded. "Since I was fourteen. And I let him. I never disagreed with anything he said, even when I didn't think he was right." She traced a pattern on the metal fence. "I saw what I could have become last Saturday. He brought his newest girlfriend over to show me. She thought I was the hired help and treated me accordingly. We had words. Lots of words. Now I'm not speaking to J.B."

He leaned back against the gate. "You may not believe it, but standing up to people is the only way to get through life with your mind intact. Nothing was ever gained by giving in."

"So that's how you left the army, is it?" she mused.

He laughed curtly. "Our commanding officer sent us against an enemy company, understrength, without proper body armor, with weapons that were misfiring. I took exception and he called me a name I didn't like. I decked him, wrapped him up in his blanket and gagged him, and led the attack myself. Tactics brought us all back alive. His way would have wiped us out to the last man. The brass didn't approve of my methods, so I had the choice of being honorably discharged or court-martialed. It was a close decision," he added with cold humor.

She just stared at him. "How could they do that? Send you into battle without proper equipment . . . That's outrageous!"

"Talk to Congress," he said coolly. "But don't expect them to do anything, unless it's an election year. Improvements cost money. We don't have enough."

She stared out over the distant pasture. "What happened to your commanding officer?"

"Oh, they promoted him," he said. "Called his tactics brilliant, in fact."

"But he didn't go, and they were your tactics!" she exclaimed.

He raised an eyebrow. "That's not what he told the brass."

She glowered. "Somebody should have told them!"

"In fact, just last week one of his execs got drunk enough to spill the beans to a reporter for one of the larger newspaper chains. A court-martial board is convening in the near future, or so I hear."

"Will they call you to testify?" she wondered.

He smiled. "God, I hope so," he replied.

She laughed at his expression. "Revenge is sweet?"

"So they tell me. Being of a naturally sweet and retiring disposition, I rarely ever cause problems . . . why are you laughing?"

She was almost doubled over. He was the last man she could picture that way.

"Maybe I caused a little trouble, once in a while," he had to admit. He glanced at his watch. "Lunch break's over. Better get back to work, so that Justin doesn't start looking for replacements."

"It was a nice lunch break, even if we didn't eat anything."

"I wasn't hungry. Sorry, I didn't think about food."

She smiled up at him. "Neither did I. We had a big breakfast this morning, and I was stuffed. Wouldn't you like to come over for pizza tonight?"

He hesitated. "I would, but I'm not going to."

"Why?"

"I'm not going to provide any more reasons for Hammock to take out old injuries on you."

"I'm not afraid of J.B."

"Neither am I," he agreed. "But let's give him time to calm down before we start any more trouble."

"I suppose we could," she agreed, but reluctantly. She didn't want J.B. to think she was bowing down to him.

The weekend went smoothly. J.B. and his blond appendage were nowhere in sight, and neither was Grange. Tellie played Monopoly with Marge and the girls on Saturday night, and went to church with them on Sunday morning.

Monday morning, Marge didn't get up for breakfast. Tellie took her a tray, worried because she seemed unusually pale and languorous.

"Just a little dizziness and nausea, Tellie," Marge protested with a wan smile. "I'll stay in bed and feel better. Really. The girls are here if I need help."

"You'd better call me if you do," she said firmly.

Marge smiled and nodded. Tellie noticed an odd rhythm in her heartbeat—it was so strong that it was shaking her nightgown. Nausea and an erratic heartbeat were worrisome symptoms. Tellie's grandfather had died of heart trouble, and she remembered the same symptoms in him.

She didn't make a big deal out of it, but she did put aside her hurt pride long enough to drive by J.B.'s office on the way to the feedlot.

He was talking to a visiting cattleman, but when he saw Tellie, he broke off the conversation politely and joined her in the outer office. He looked good in jeans and a chambray shirt and chaps, she thought, even if they were designer clothing. He was working today, not squiring around women.

"Couldn't stand it anymore, I gather?" he asked curtly. "You just had to come and see me and apologize?"

She frowned. "Excuse me?"

"It's about time," he told her. "But I'm busy today. You should have picked a better time."

"J.B., I need to talk to you," she began.

He gave her slender figure in the green pantsuit a curiously intent scrutiny, winding his way back up the modest neckline to her face, with only the lightest touch of makeup, and her wavy hair like a dark cap around her head. "On your way to work?"

"Yes," she said. "J.B., I have to tell you something . . ."

He took her arm and led her back outside to her car. "Later. I've got a full day. Besides," he added as he opened her car door, "you know I don't like to be chased. I like to do the chasing."

She let out an exasperated breath. "J.B., I'm not chasing you! If you'd just give me a chance to speak . . . !"

His eyes narrowed. "I don't like treating you like the enemy, but I also don't like the way you spoke to Bella. When you apologize, to her, we'll go from there."

"Apologize?"

His face hardened. "You took too much for granted. You aren't part of my family, and you aren't a lover. You can't treat my women like trespassers in my own sister's house. Maybe we were close, when you were younger, but that's over."

"She started it," she began, riled.

"She belongs with me. You don't." His eyes were hard. "I need more from a woman than a handshake at the end of the evening. That's as much as you're able to give, Tellie. You're completely unawakened."

She wondered what he was talking about. But she didn't have time to ponder enigmas. "Listen, Bella's not what I came here to talk about!"

"I'm not giving up Bella," he continued, as if she hadn't spoken. "And chasing after me like this isn't going to get you anything except the wrong side of my temper. Don't do it again."

"J.B.!"

He closed the door. "Go to work," he said shortly, and turned away.

Of all the arrogant, assuming, overbearing conceited jackasses, she thought as she reversed out of the parking space and took off toward town, he took the cake. She wasn't chasing him, she was trying to tell him about Marge! Well, she could try again later. Next time, she promised herself, she'd make him listen.

She walked in the front door after work, tired and dispirited. Maybe Marge was better, she hoped.

"Tellie, is that you?" Dawn exclaimed from the top of the staircase. "Come on up. Hurry, please!"

Tellie took the steps two at a time. Marge was lying on her back, gasping for breath, wincing with pain. Her face was a grayish tone, her skin cold and clammy.

"Heart attack," Tellie said at once. She'd seen this all

before, with her grandfather. She grabbed the phone and dialed 911.

She tried to call J.B., but she couldn't get an answer on his cell phone, or on the phone at the office or his house. She waited until the ambulance loaded up Marge, and the girls went with her, to get into her car and drive to J.B.'s house. If she couldn't find him, she could at least get Nell to relay a message.

She leaped out of the car and ran to the front door. She tried the knob and found it unlocked. This was no time for formality. She opened it and ran down the hall to J.B.'s study. She threw open the door and stopped dead in the doorway.

J.B. looked up, over Bella's bare white shoulders, his face flushed, his mouth swollen, his shirt off.

"What the hell are you doing here?" he demanded furiously.

Six

Tellie could barely get her breath. Worried about Marge, half-sick with fear, she couldn't even manage words. No wonder J.B. couldn't be bothered to answer the phone. He and his beautiful girlfriend were half-naked. Apparently J.B. wasn't much on beds for his sensual adventures. She remembered with heartache that he'd wrestled her down on that very sofa when she was eighteen and kissed her until her mouth hurt. It had been the most heavenly few minutes of her entire life, despite the fact that he'd been furious when he started kissing her. It hadn't ended that way, though . . .

"Get out!" J.B. threw at her.

She managed to get her wits back. Marge. She had to think about Marge, not about how much her pride was hurting. "J.B., you have to listen . . ."

"Get out, damn you!" he raged. "I've had it up to here with you chasing after me, pawing me, trying to get close to me! I don't want you, Tellie, how many times do I have to tell you before you realize that I mean it? You're a stray that Marge and I took in, nothing more! I don't want you, and I never will!"

Her heart was bursting with raw pain. She hoped she wouldn't pass out. She knew her face was white. She wanted to move, to leave, but her feet felt frozen to the carpet.

Her tormented expression and lack of response seemed to make him worse. "You skinny, ugly little tomboy," he raged, white-hot with fury. "Who'd want something like you for keeps? Get out, I said!"

She gave up. She turned away, slowly, aware of the gloating smile on Bella's face, and closed the door behind her. Her knees barely gave her support as she walked back toward the front door.

Nell was standing by the staircase, drying her hands on her apron, looking shocked. "What in the world is all the yelling about?" she exclaimed. She hesitated when she saw the younger woman's drawn, white face. "Tellie, what's wrong?" she asked gently.

Tellie fought for composure. "Marge . . . is on her

way to the hospital in an ambulance, with the girls. I think it's a heart attack. I couldn't make J.B. listen. He's . . . I walked in on him and that woman . . . He yelled at me and said I was chasing him, and called me horrible names . . . !" She swallowed hard and drew herself erect. "Please tell him we'll all be at the hospital, if he can tear himself loose long enough!"

She turned toward the door.

"Don't you drive that car unless you're all right, Tellie," Nell said firmly. "It's pouring down rain."

"I'm fine," she said in a ghostly tone. She even forced a smile. "Tell him, okay?"

"I'll tell him," Nell said angrily. Her voice softened. "Don't worry, honey. Marge is one tough cookie. She'll be all right. You just drive carefully. You ought to wait and go with him," she added slowly.

"If I got in a car with him right now, I'd kill him," Tellie said through her teeth. Helpless tears were rolling down her pale cheeks. "See you later, Nell."

"Tellie . . ."

It was too late. Tellie closed the door behind her and went to her car. She was getting soaked and she didn't care. J.B. had said terrible things to her. She knew that she'd never get over them. He wanted her to stop chasing him. She hadn't been, but it must have looked like it. She'd gone to his office this morning, and to the house this afternoon. It was about Marge. He wouldn't believe it, though. He thought Tellie was desperate for him. That was a joke, now. She was sure that she never wanted to see him again as long as she lived.

She started the car and turned it. The tires were slick. She hadn't realized how slick until she almost spun out going down the driveway. She needed to keep her speed down, but she wasn't thinking rationally. She was hearing J.B. yell at her that she was an ugly stray he'd taken in, that he didn't want her. Tears misted her eyes as she tried to concentrate on the road.

There was a hairpin curve just before the ranch road met the highway. It was usually easy to maneuver, but the rain was coming so hard and fast that the little car suddenly hydroplaned. She saw the ditch coming toward her and jerked the wheel as hard as she could. In a daze, she felt the car go over and over and over. Her seat belt broke and something hit her head. Everything went black.

J.B. stormed out of the living room just seconds after he heard Tellie's little car scatter gravel as it sped away. His hair was mussed, like his shirt, and he was in a vicious humor. It had been a bad day altogether. He shouldn't have yelled at Tellie. But he wondered why she'd come barging in. He should have asked. It was just that it had shamed him to be seen in such a position with Bella, knowing painfully how Tellie felt about him. He'd hurt her with just the sight of him and Bella, without adding his scathing comments afterward. Tellie wouldn't even realize that shame had put him on the offensive. She had feelings of glass, and he'd shattered them.

Nell was waiting for him at the foot of the staircase.

She was visibly seething, and her white hair almost stood on end with bridled rage. "So you finally came out, did you?"

"Tellie was tearing up the driveway as she left," he bit off. "What the hell got into her? Why was she here?" he added reluctantly, because he'd realized, belatedly, that she hadn't looked as if she were pursuing him with amorous intent.

Nell gave him a cold smile. "She couldn't get you on the phone, so she drove over to tell you that Marge has had a heart attack." She nodded curtly when she saw him turn pale. "That's right. She wasn't here chasing you. She wanted you to know about your sister."

"Oh, God," he bit off.

"*He* won't help you," Nell ground out. "Yelling at poor Tellie like that, when she was only trying to do you a good turn . . . !"

"Shut up," he snapped angrily. "Call the hospital and see . . ."

"You call them." She took off her apron. "You've got my two weeks' notice, as of right now. I'm sick of watching you torture Tellie. I quit! See if your harpy girlfriend in there can cook your meals and clean your house while she spends you into the poorhouse!"

"Nell," he began furiously.

She held up a hand. "I won't reconsider."

The living room door opened, and Bella slinked into the hallway, smiling contentedly. "Aren't we going out to eat?" she asked J.B. as she moved to catch him by one arm.

"I'm going to the hospital," he said. "My sister's had a heart attack."

"Oh, that's too bad," Bella said. "Do you want me to go with you and hold your hand?"

"The girls will love that," Nell said sarcastically. "You'll be such a comfort to them!"

"Nell!" J.B. fumed.

"She's right, I'd be a comfort, like she said," Bella agreed, missing the sarcasm altogether. "You need me, J.B."

"I hope he gets what he really needs one day," Nell said, turning on her heel.

"You're fired!" he yelled after her.

"Too late, I already quit," Nell said pleasantly. "I'm sure Bella can cook you some supper and wash your clothes." She closed the kitchen door behind her with a snap.

"Now, you know I can't cook, J.B.," Bella said irritably. "And I've never washed clothes—I send mine to the laundry. What's the matter with her? It's that silly girl who was here, isn't it? I don't like her at all . . ."

J.B. reached into his pocket and pulled out two large bills. "Call a cab and go home," he said shortly. "I have to get to the hospital."

"But I should go with you," she argued.

He looked down at her with bridled fury. "Go home."

She shifted restlessly. "Well, all right, J.B., you don't need to yell. Honestly, you're in such a bad mood!"

"My sister has had a heart attack," he repeated.

"Yes, I know, but those things happen, don't they?

You can't do anything about it," she added blankly.

It was like talking to a wall, he thought with exasperation. He tucked in his shirt, checked to make sure his car keys were in his pocket, jerked his raincoat and hat from the hall coat rack and went out the door without a backward glance.

Dawn and Brandi were pacing the waiting room in the emergency room at Jacobsville General Hospital while Dr. Coltrain examined their mother. They were quiet, somber, with tears pouring down their cheeks in silent misery when J.B. walked in.

They ran to him the instant they saw him, visibly shaken. He gathered them close, feeling like an animal because he hadn't even let Tellie talk when she'd walked in on him. She'd come to tell him that Marge was in the hospital with a heart attack, and he'd sent her running with insults. Probably she'd come to his office that morning because something about Marge had worried her. He'd been no help at all. Now Tellie was hurt and Nell was quitting. He'd never felt so helpless.

"Mama won't die, will she, Uncle J.B.?" Brandi asked tearfully.

"Of course she won't," he assured her in the deep, soft tone he used with little things or hurt children. "She'll be fine."

"Tellie said she was going to tell you about Mama. Why didn't Tellie come with you?" Dawn asked, wiping her eyes.

He stiffened. "Tellie's not here?"

"No. She had to go over to your house, because you didn't answer your phone," Brandi replied. "I guess the lines were down or something."

"Or something," he said huskily. He'd taken the phone off the hook.

"She may have gone home to get Mama a gown," Dawn suggested. "She always thinks of things like that, when everybody else goes to pieces."

"She'll be here as soon as she can . . . I know she will," Brandi agreed. "I don't know what we'd do without Tellie."

Which made J.B. feel even smaller than he already did. Tellie must be scared to death. She'd been with her grandfather when he died of a heart attack. She'd loved him more than any other member of her small family, including the mother she'd lost more recently. Marge's heart attack would bring back terrible memories. Worse, when she showed up at the hospital, she'd have to deal with what J.B. had said to her. It wasn't going to be a pleasant reunion.

Dr. Coltrain came out, smiling. "Marge is going to be all right," he told them. "We got to her just in time. But she'll have to see a heart specialist, and she's going to be on medication from now on. Did you know that her blood pressure was high?"

"No!" J.B. said at once. "It's always been low!"

Coltrain shook his head. "Not anymore. She's very lucky that it happened like this. It may have saved her life."

"It was a heart attack, then?" J.B. persisted, with the girls standing close at his side.

"Yes. But a mild one. You can see her when we've got her in a room. You'll need to sign her in at the office."

"I'll do that right now."

"But, where's Tellie?" Dawn asked when they were alone.

J.B. wished he knew.

He was on his way back from the office when he passed the emergency room, just in time to see a worried Grange stalking in beside a gurney that two paramedics were rushing through the door. On the stretcher was Tellie, unconscious and bleeding.

"Tellie!" he exclaimed, rushing to the gurney. She was white as a sheet, and he was more frightened now than he was when he learned about Marge. "What happened?" he shot at Grange.

"I don't know," Grange said curtly. "Her car was off the road in a ditch. She was unconscious, in a couple of inches of water, facedown. If I hadn't come along when I did, she'd have drowned."

J.B. felt sick all the way to his soul. It was his fault. All his fault. "Where was the car?" he asked.

"On the farm road that leads to your house," Grange replied, his eyes narrowed, suspiciously. "Why are you here?"

"My sister just had a heart attack," he said solemnly. "The girls and I have been in the emergency waiting room. She's going to be all right. Tellie came to tell me about it," he added reluctantly.

"Then why in hell didn't she ride in with you?" Grange asked, brown eyes flashing. "She must have been upset—she loves Marge. She shouldn't even have been driving in weather this dangerous."

That was a question J.B. didn't want to touch. He ignored it, following the gurney into one of the examination rooms with Grange right on his heels.

He got one of Tellie's small hands in both of his and held on tight. "Tellie," he said huskily, feeling the pain all the way to his boots. "Tellie, hold on!"

"She shouldn't have been driving," Grange repeated, leaning against the wall nearby. He was obviously upset as well, and the look he gave J.B. would have started a fight under better circumstances.

The entrance of Copper Coltrain interrupted him.

Copper gave J.B. an odd look. "It isn't your day, is it?" he asked, moving to Tellie's side. "What happened?"

"Her car hydroplaned, apparently," Grange said tautly. "I found it overturned. She was lying facedown in a ditch full of water. If I'd been just a little later, she'd have drowned."

"Damn the luck!" Coltrain muttered, checking her pupil reaction with a small penlight. "She's concussed as well as bruised," he murmured. "I'm going to need X-rays and a battery of tests to see how badly she's hurt. But the concussion is the main thing."

J.B. felt sick. One of his men had been kicked in the head by a mean steer and dropped dead of a massive concussion. "Can't you do something now?" he raged at Coltrain.

The physician gave him an odd look. It was notorious gossip locally that Tellie was crazy about J. B. Hammock, and that J.B. paid her as little attention as possible. The white-faced man with blazing green eyes facing him didn't seem disinterested.

"What would you suggest?" he asked J.B. curtly.

"Wake her up!"

Grange made a rough sound in his throat.

"You can shut up," J.B. told him icily. "You're not a doctor."

"Neither are you," Grange returned with the same lack of warmth. "And if you'd given her a lift to the hospital, she wouldn't need one, would she?"

J.B. had already worked that out for himself. His lips compressed furiously.

Tellie groaned.

Both men moved to the examination table at the same time. Coltrain gave them angry looks and bent to examine Tellie.

"Can you hear me?" he asked her softly. "Tellie?"

Her eyes opened, green and dazed. She blinked and winced. "My head hurts."

"I'm not surprised," Coltrain murmured, busy with a stethoscope. "Take a deep breath. Let it out. Again."

She groaned. "My head hurts," she repeated.

"Okay, I'll give you something for it. But we need X-rays and an MRI," Coltrain said quietly. "Anything hurt besides your head?"

"Everything," she replied. "What happened?"

"You wrecked your car," Grange said quietly.

She looked up at him. "You found me?"

He nodded, dark eyes concerned.

She managed a smile. "Thanks." She shivered. "I'm wet!"

"It was pouring rain," Grange said, his voice soft, like his eyes. He brushed back the blood-matted hair from her forehead, disclosing a growing dark bruise. He winced.

"You're concussed, Tellie," Dr. Coltrain said. "We're going to have to keep you for a day or two. Okay?"

"But I'll miss graduation!" she exclaimed, trying to sit up.

He gently pushed her back down. "No, you won't," he said with a quizzical smile.

She blinked, glancing at J.B., who looked very worried. "But it's May. I'm a senior. I have a white gown and cap." She hesitated. "Was I driving Marge's car?"

"No. Your own," J.B. said slowly, apprehensively.

"But I don't have a car, don't you remember, J.B.?" she asked pleasantly. "I have to drive Marge's. She's going to help me buy a car this summer, because I'm going to work at the Sav-A-Lot Grocery Store, remember?"

J.B.'s indrawn breath was audible. Before the other two men could react, he pressed Tellie's small hand closer in his own. "Tellie, how old are you?" he asked.

"I'm seventeen, you know that," she scoffed.

Coltrain whistled. J.B. turned to him, his lips parted

in the preliminary to a question.

"We're going to step outside and discuss how to break it to Marge," Coltrain told her gently. "You just rest. I'll send a nurse in with something for your headache, okay?"

"Okay," she agreed. "J.B., you aren't leaving, are you?" she added worriedly.

Coals of fire, he was thinking, as he assured her that he'd be nearby. She relaxed and smiled as she lay back on the examination table.

Coltrain motioned the other two men outside into the hall. "Amnesia," he told J.B. at once. "I'm sure it's temporary," he added quickly. "It isn't uncommon with head injuries. She's very confused, and in some pain. I'll run tests. We'll do an MRI to make sure."

"The head injury would cause it?" Grange asked worriedly.

J.B. had a flush along his high cheekbones. He didn't speak.

Coltrain gave him a curious look. "The brain tends to try to protect itself from trauma, and not only physical trauma. Has she had a shock of some kind?" he asked J.B. pointedly.

J.B. replied with a curt jerk of his head. "We had a . . . misunderstanding at the house," he admitted.

Grange's dark eyes flashed. "Well, that explains why she wrecked the car!" he accused.

J.B. glared at him. "Like hell it does . . . !"

Coltrain held up a hand. "Arguing isn't going to do her any good. She's had the wreck, now we have to deal with the consequences. I'm going to admit her and start running tests."

J.B. drew a quick breath. "How are we going to explain this to Tellie?"

Coltrain sighed. "Tell her as little as possible, right now. Once she's stabilized, we'll tell her what we have to. But if she thinks she's seventeen, sending her to Marge's house is going to be traumatic—she'll expect the girls to be four years younger than they are, won't she?"

J.B. was thinking, hard. He saw immediately a way to solve that problem and prevent Nell from escaping at once. "She can stay at the house with Nell and me," he said. "She and Marge and the girls did stay there when she was seventeen for a couple of weeks while Marge's house was being remodeled. We can tell her that Marge and the girls are having a vacation while workmen tend to her house. I'll make it right with Dawn and Brandi."

"You and Tellie were close when she was in her teens, I recall," Coltrain recalled.

"Yes," J.B. said tautly.

Coltrain chuckled, glancing at Grange. "She followed him around like a puppy when she first went to live with Marge," he told the other man. "You couldn't talk to J.B. without tripping over Tellie. J.B. was her security blanket after she lost her mother."

"She was the same way with Marge," J.B. muttered.

"Not to that extent, she wasn't," Coltrain argued. "She thought the sun rose and set on you . . ."

"I need to go back and check on Marge," J.B. interrupted, visibly uncomfortable.

"I'll stay with Tellie for a while," Grange said, moving back into the examination room before the other two men could object.

J.B. stared after him with bridled fury, his hands deep in his pockets, his eyes smoldering. "He's got no business in there," he told Coltrain. "He isn't even family!"

"Neither are you," the doctor reminded him.

J.B. glared at him. "Are you sure she'll be all right?"

"As sure as I can be." He studied the other man intently. "You said something to her, something that hurt, didn't you?" he asked, nodding when J.B.'s high cheekbones took on a ruddy color. "She's hiding in the past, when you were less resentful of her. She'll get her memory back, but it's going to be dangerous to rush it. You have to let her move ahead at her own pace."

"I'll do that," J.B. assured him. He drew in a long breath. "Damn. I feel as if my whole life crashed and burned today. First Marge, now Tellie. And Nell quit," he added angrily.

"Nell?" Coltrain exclaimed. "She's been there since you were a boy."

"Well, she wants to leave," J.B. muttered. "But she'll stay if she knows Tellie's coming to the house. I'd better phone her. Then I'll go back to Marge's room." He met Coltrain's eyes. "If she needs anything, *anything,* I'll take care of it. I don't think she's got any health insurance at all."

"You might stop by the admissions office and set things up," Coltrain suggested. "But I'll do what needs doing, finances notwithstanding. You know that."

"I do. Thanks, Copper."

Coltrain shrugged. "I'm glad she's rallying," he said. "And Marge, too."

"Same here."

J.B. left him to go back to the admissions office and sign Tellie in. He felt guilty. Her wreck was certainly his fault. The least he could do was provide for her treatment. He hated knowing that he'd upset her that much, and for nothing. She was only trying to help. Frustration had taken its toll on him and driven him into Bella's willing arms. The last thing he'd expected was for Tellie to walk in on them. He'd never been quite so ashamed of himself. Which was, of course, no excuse to take his temper out on her. He wished he could take back all the things he'd said. While her memory was gone, at least he had a chance to regain her trust and make up, a little, for what he'd done.

Tellie felt drained by the time Coltrain had all the tests he wanted. She was curious about the man who'd told her that he found her in the wrecked car and called the ambulance. He was handsome and friendly and seemed to like her very much, but she didn't know him.

"It was very kind of you to rescue me," she told Grange when she was in a private room.

He shrugged. "My pleasure." He smiled at her, his dark eyes twinkling. "You can save me, next time."

She laughed. Her head cocked to one side as she studied him. "I'm sorry, but I don't remember your name."

"Grange," he said pleasantly.

"Just Grange?" she queried.

He nodded.

"Have I known you a long time?"

He shook his head. "But I've taken you out a few times."

Her eyebrows lifted. "And J.B. let me go with you?" she exclaimed. "That's very strange. I wanted to go hiking with a college boy I knew and he threw a fit. You're older than any college boy."

He chuckled. "I'm twenty-seven," he told her.

"Wow," she mused.

"You're old for your age," he said, evading her eyes. "J.B. and I know each other."

"I see." She didn't, but he was obviously reluctant to talk about it. "Marge hasn't been to see me," she added suddenly. "That's not like her."

Grange recalled what J.B. and Coltrain had discussed. "Her house is being remodeled," he said. "She and the girls are on a vacation trip."

"While school's in session?" she exclaimed.

He thought fast. "It's Spring Break, remember?"

She was confused. Hadn't someone said it was May? Wasn't Spring Break in March? "But graduation is coming up very soon."

"You got your cap and gown early, didn't you?" he improvised.

She was frowning. "That must be what happened. I'm so confused," she murmured, holding her head. "And my head absolutely throbs."

"They'll give you something for that." He checked his watch. "I have to go. Visiting hours are over."

"Will you come back tomorrow?" she asked, feeling deserted.

He smiled. "Of course I will." He hesitated. "It will have to be during my lunch hour, or after work, though."

"Where do you work?"

"At the Ballenger feedlot."

That set off bells in her head, but she couldn't think why. "They're nice, Justin and Calhoun."

"Yes, they are." He stood up, moving the chair back from her bed. "Take care. I'll see you tomorrow."

"Okay. Thanks again."

He looked at her for a long time. "I'm glad it wasn't more serious than it is," he told her. "You were unconscious when I found you."

"It was raining," she recalled hesitantly. "I don't understand why I was driving in the rain. I'm afraid of it, you know."

"Are you?"

She shook her head. "I must have had a reason."

"I'm sure you did." He looked thunderous, but he quickly erased the expression, smiled and left her.

She settled back into the pillow, feeling bruised and broken. It was such an odd experience, what had happened to her. Everyone seemed to be holding things back from her. She wondered how badly she was damaged. Tomorrow, she promised herself, she'd dig it out of J.B.

Seven

Tellie woke up early, expecting to find herself alone. But J.B. was sprawled in the chair next to the bed, snoring faintly, and he looked as if he'd been there for some time. A nurse was tiptoeing around to get Tellie's vitals, sending amused and interested glances at the long, lean cowboy beside the bed.

"Has he been there long?" Tellie wanted to know.

"Since daybreak," the nurse replied with a smile. She put the electronic thermometer in Tellie's ear, let it beep, checked it and wrote down a figure. She checked her pulse and recorded that, as well. "I understand the nurse on the last shift tried to evict him and the hospital administrator actually came down here in person to tell her to cease and desist." She gave Tellie a speaking glance. "I gather that your visitor is somebody very important."

"He paid for that MRI machine they used on me yesterday."

The nurse pursed her lips. "Well! Aren't you nicely connected?" she mused. "Is he your fiancé?"

Tellie chuckled. "I'm only seventeen," she said.

The nurse looked puzzled. She checked Tellie's chart, made a face and then forced a smile. "Of course. Sorry."

Tellie wondered why she looked so confused. "Can I go home today?" she wondered.

"That depends on what Dr. Coltrain thinks," she

replied. "He'll be in to see you when he makes rounds. Breakfast will be up shortly."

"Thanks," Tellie told her.

The nurse smiled, cast another curious and appreciative glance at J.B. and left.

Tellie stared at him with mixed emotions. He was a handsome man, she thought, but at least she was safe from all that masculine charm that he used to such good effect on women he liked. She was far too young to be threatened by J.B.'s sex appeal.

It was easy to see why he had women flocking around him. He had a dynamite physique, hard and lean and sexy, with long powerful legs and big hands. His face was rugged, but he had fine green eyes under a jutting brow and a mouth that was as hard and sensuous as any movie star's. But it wasn't just his looks that made him attractive. It was his voice, deep and faintly raspy, and the way he had of making a woman feel special. He had beautiful manners when he cared to display them, and a temper that made grown men look for cover. Tellie had rarely seen him fighting mad. Most of the time he had excellent self-control.

She frowned. Why did it sting to think of him losing his temper? He'd rarely lost it at Tellie, and even then it was for her own good. But something about her thoughts made her uneasy.

Just as she was focusing on that, J.B. opened his eyes and looked at her, and she stopped thinking. Her heart jumped. She couldn't imagine why. She was possessive of J.B., she idolized him, but she'd never really considered anything physical between them. Now, her body seemed to know things her mind didn't.

"How do you feel?" he asked quietly.

She blinked. "My head doesn't hurt as much," she said. She searched his eyes. "Why are you here? I'm all right."

He shrugged. "I was worried." He didn't add that he was also guilt-ridden about the reason for the wreck and her injury. His conscience had him on the rack. He couldn't sleep for worrying about her. That was new. It was disconcerting. He'd never let a woman get under his skin since his ill-fated romance of years past. Even an unexpected interlude with Tellie on the sofa in his office hadn't made a lot of difference in their turbulent relationship, especially when he realized that Tellie was sexually unawakened. He'd deliberately pushed her out of his life and kept her at arm's length—well, mostly, except for unavoidable lapses when he gave in to the passion riding him. That passion had drawn him to Bella in a moment of weakness.

Then Tellie had walked in on him with Bella, and his whole life had changed. He'd never felt such pain as when Grange had walked into the emergency room with an unconscious Tellie on a gurney. Nothing was ever going to be the same again. The only thing worse than seeing her in such a condition was dreading the day when her memory returned, because she was going to hate J.B.

"I'm going to be fine," she promised, smiling. "Do you think Dr. Coltrain will let me go home today?"

"I'll ask him," he said, sitting up straighter. "Nell's getting a room ready for you. While Marge and the girls are away, you'll stay with Nell and me."

"I wish Marge was here," she said involuntarily.

He sighed. Marge was improving, too, but she was worried about Tellie. Dawn had let it slip that she'd been in a wreck, but J.B. had assured her that Tellie was going to be fine. There was this little problem with her memory, of course, and she'd have to stay at the house with him until it came back.

Marge was reassured, but still concerned. He knew that she'd sensed something was wrong between her brother and Tellie, but she couldn't put it into words. He wasn't about to enlighten her. He had enough on his plate.

"I'll be in the way there," she protested.

"You won't," he replied. "Nell will be glad of the company."

She studied her hands on the sheet. "There's something that bothers me, J.B.," she said without looking at him.

"What?"

She hesitated. "What was I doing at your house, at night, in the rain?"

He sat very still. He hadn't considered that the question would arise so soon. He wasn't sure how to answer it, to protect her from painful memories.

She looked up and met his turbulent green eyes. "You were mad at me, weren't you?"

His heart seemed to stop, then start again. "We had an argument," he began slowly.

She nodded. "I thought so. But I can't remember what it was about."

"Time enough for that when you're back on your feet," he said, rising up from the chair. "Don't borrow trouble. Just get well."

So there was something! She wished she could grasp what it was. J.B. was acting very oddly.

She looked up at him. "You leaving?" she asked.

He nodded. "I've got to get the boys started moving the bulls to summer pasture."

"Not on roundup?"

"Roundup's in March," he said easily.

"Oh." She frowned. It wasn't March. She knew it wasn't. "Is it March?"

He ignored that. "I'll talk to Coltrain on my way out," he said.

"But it's not time for rounds . . ."

"I met him coming in. He had an emergency surgery. I expect he's through by now," he replied.

"J.B., who is that man Grange?" she asked abruptly. "And why did you let me go out with him? He said he's twenty-seven, and I'm just seventeen. You had a hissy fit when I tried to go hiking with Billy Johns."

He looked indignant. "I don't have hissy fits," he said shortly.

"Well, you raged at me, anyway," she corrected. "Why are you letting me see Grange?"

His teeth set. "You're full of questions this morning."

"Answer a few of them," she invited.

"Later," he said, deliberately checking his watch. "I

have to get to work. Want me to bring you anything?"

"A nail file and a ladder," she said with resignation. "Just get me out of here."

"The minute you're fit to leave," he promised. He smiled faintly. "Stay put until I get back."

"If I must," she sighed.

He was gone and she was left to eat breakfast and while away the next few hours until Dr. Coltrain showed up.

He examined Tellie and pronounced her fit to leave the hospital.

"But you still need to take it easy for a week or two," he told her. "Stay out of crowds, stick to J.B.'s house. No parties, no job, nothing."

She frowned. "I thought it was just a mild concussion," she argued.

"It is." He didn't quite meet her eyes. "We're just not taking chances. You need lots of rest."

She sighed. "Okay, if you say so. Can I go horseback riding, can I swim . . . ?"

"Sure. Just don't leave J.B.'s ranch to do them."

She smiled. "What's going on, Dr. Coltrain?"

He leaned forward. "It's a secret," he told her. "Bear with me. Okay?"

She laughed. "Okay. When do I get to know the secret?"

"All in good time," he added, as inspiration struck him. "Keep an eye on J.B. for me."

Her eyebrows arched. "Is something wrong with him . . . ?" she asked worriedly.

"Nothing specific. Just watch him."

She shook her head. "Okay. If you say so."

"Good girl." He patted her shoulder and left, congratulating himself on the inspiration. While she was focused on J.B., she wouldn't be preoccupied with her own health. Far better if she licked the amnesia all by herself. He didn't want her shocked with the truth of her condition.

J.B.'s house was bigger than Tellie remembered. Nell met them at the door, all smiles and welcome.

"It's so good to have you back," Nell said, hugging the younger woman. "I've got a nice room all ready for you."

"Don't think you're going to get to wait on me," Tellie informed her with a grin. "I'm not an invalid."

"You have a concussion," Nell corrected, and the smile faded. "It can be very dangerous. I remember a cowboy who worked here . . ."

"Remember us something to eat, instead," J.B. interrupted her, with a meaningful look.

"Oh. Of course." She glared at J.B. "You had a call while you were out. I wrote the information on the pad on your desk."

He read through the lines and assumed it was from Bella. "I'll take care of it."

"Who's bringing Tellie's suitcase?" Nell asked.

J.B. stood still. "What suitcase?"

"I'll have to go over to Marge's and get my things," Tellie began.

"I'll go—!"

"I can do that," J.B. interrupted Nell. "You look after Tellie."

"When haven't I?" Nell wanted to know belligerently.

"You two need to stop arguing, or I'm going to go sit on the front porch," Tellie told both of them.

They glared at each other. J.B. shrugged and went into his den. Tellie's eyes followed him past the big sofa. The sofa . . . She frowned. Something about that sofa made her uneasy.

"What's wrong?" Nell prompted.

Tellie put a hand to her forehead and laughed faintly. "I don't know. I looked at the sofa and felt funny."

"Let's go right up and get you settled," Nell said abruptly, taking Tellie by the arm. "Then I'll see about some lunch."

It was almost as if Nell knew something about the sofa, too, but that would be ridiculous, Tellie told herself. She was getting mental.

She'd wanted to watch television, but there wasn't one in the bedroom. Nell told her that there was a problem with the satellite dish and it wasn't working. Odd, Tellie thought, it was almost as if they were trying to keep her from watching the news.

She had to stay in bed, because Nell insisted. Just after she had supper on a tray, J.B. walked in, worn and dusty, still in his working clothes.

Tellie was propped up in bed in pink-striped pajamas

that made her look oddly vulnerable.

"How's it going?" he asked.

"I'm okay. Why is the satellite not working?" she added. "I can't watch the Weather Channel."

His eyebrows arched. "Why do you want to?"

"You said it was March, but Nell says it's May," she said. "That's tornado season."

"So it is."

She glowered at him. "Grange said it was March and Marge and the girls were away on Spring Break."

He pursed his lips.

"I know better, so don't bother trying to lie," she told him firmly. "If it's May, where are they?"

He leaned against the doorjamb. "They're around, but you can't see them just yet. Nothing's wrong."

"That's not true, J.B.," she said flatly.

He laughed mirthlessly and twirled his hat through his fingers. "No use trying to fool you, is it? Okay, the concussion did something to your head. You're a little fuzzy about things. We're supposed to let your mind clear without any help."

She frowned. "What's fuzzy about it?"

He jerked away from the door. "Not tonight. I'm going to clean up, then I've got . . . someplace to go," he amended.

"A date," she translated, grinning.

There was faint jealousy in her expression, but she was hiding it very well. He felt uncomfortable. He was taking Bella out, and here was Tellie, badly injured on his account and hurting.

"I could postpone it," he began guiltily.

"Whatever for?" she exclaimed.

His eyebrows arched. "Excuse me?"

"I'm seventeen," she pointed out. "Even if I were crazy about you, it's obvious that you're far too old for me."

He felt odd inside. He studied her curiously. "Am I?"

"I still don't understand why you're letting Grange date me," she mused. "He's twenty-seven."

"Is he?" He considered that. Grange was seven years his junior, closer to Tellie's own age than he was. That stung.

"You're hedging, J.B.," she accused.

He checked his watch. "Maybe so. I've got to go. Nell will be here if you need anything."

"I won't."

He turned to go, hesitated, and looked back at her, brooding. If she tried the television sets, she'd discover that they all worked. "Don't wander around the house."

She gaped at him. "Why would I want to?"

"Just don't. I'll see you tomorrow."

She watched him go, curious about his odd behavior.

Later, she tried to pump Nell for information, but it was like talking to a wall. "You and J.B. are stonewalling me," she accused.

Nell smiled. "For a good cause. Just relax and enjoy being here, for the time that's left." She picked up the empty iced-tea glass on the bedside table, looking around the room. "Odd that J.B. would put you in here," she said, thinking aloud.

"Is it? Why?"

"It was his grandmother's room," she said with a smile. "She was a wonderful old lady. J.B. adored her. She'd been an actress in Hollywood in her youth. She could tell some stories!"

"Does he talk about her?" Tellie wondered.

"Almost never. She died in a tornado." She nodded, at Tellie's astonished look. "That's right, one of the worst in south Texas history hit here back in the eighties," she recalled. "It lifted the barn off its foundations and twisted it. His grandmother's favorite horse was trapped there, and old Mrs. Hammock put on a raincoat and rushed out to try to save it. Nobody saw her go. The tornado picked her up and put her in the top of an oak tree, dead. They had to get a truck with a cherry picker to get her down, afterward," Nell said softly. "J.B. was watching. He hates tornadoes to this day. It's why we have elaborate storm shelters here and in the bunkhouse, and even under the barn."

"That's why he looked funny, when I mentioned liking to watch the Weather Channel," she said slowly.

"He watches it religiously in the spring and summer," Nell confided. "And he has weather alert systems in the same places he has the shelters. All his men have cell phones with alert capability. He's something of a fanatic about safety."

"Have I ever been in a tornado?" she asked Nell.

Nell looked surprised. "Why do you ask?"

"J.B. said I'm fuzzy about the past," she replied. "I gather that I've lost some memories, is that it?"

Nell came and sat down in the chair beside the bed. "Yes. You have."

"And the doctor doesn't want me remembering too soon?"

"He thinks it's better if you remember all on your own," Nell said. "So we're conspiring to keep you in the dark, so to speak," she added with a gentle smile.

Tellie frowned. "I wish I could remember what I've forgotten."

Nell burst out laughing. "Don't rush it. When you remember, we'll leave together."

Tellie gaped at her. "You're quitting? But you've been here forever!"

"I've been here too long," Nell said curtly, rising. "There are other bosses who don't yell and threaten people."

"You yell and threaten back," Tellie reminded her.

"Remembered that, did you?" she teased.

"Yes. So why are you leaving him?"

"Let's just say that I don't like his methods," she replied. "And that's all you're getting out of me. I'll be in the kitchen. Just use the intercom if you need me, okay?"

"Okay. Thanks, Nell."

Nell smiled at her. "I like having you here."

"Who's he dating this week?" Tellie called after her.

"Another stacked blonde, of course," came the dry reply. "She has the IQ of a lettuce leaf."

Tellie chuckled. "Obviously he doesn't like competition from mere women."

"Someday he'll come a cropper," she said. "I hope I live to see the day."

Tellie watched her close the door with faint misgivings. J.B. did like variety, she seemed to know that. But there was something about the reference, about a blond woman, that unsettled her. Why had she and J.B. argued? She wished she could remember.

Her light was still on when he came home. She was reading a particularly interesting book that she'd found in the bookcase, an autobiography by Libbie Custer, the woman who'd married General George Custer of Civil War and Little Bighorn fame. It was a tale of courage in the face of danger, unexpectedly riveting. Mrs. Custer, it seemed, had actually gone with her husband to the battlefield during the Civil War. Tellie had never read of women doing that. Mrs. Custer was something of a renegade for her oppressed generation, a daring and intelligent woman with a keen wit. She liked her.

J.B. opened the door to find her propped up in bed on her pillows with the book resting against her upraised knees under the covers.

"What are you doing up at this hour?" he asked sternly.

She glanced at him, still halfway in the book she was reading. He looked elegant in a dinner jacket and black tie, she thought, although the tie was in his hand and the shirt was open at the throat, over a pelt of dark hair. She frowned. Why did the sight of his bare chest make her heart race?

"I found this book on the shelf and couldn't put it down," she said.

He moved to the bed, stuck the tie in his pocket and sat down beside her. He took the book in a big, lean hand and checked the title. He gave it back, smiling. "Libbie Custer was one of my grandmother's heroines. She actually met her once, when she gave a speech in New York while my grandmother was visiting relatives there as a child. She said that Mrs. Custer was a wonderful speaker. She lived into her nineties."

"She wrote a very interesting book," Tellie said.

"There are three of them altogether," he told her. "I believe you'll find the other two on the shelf as well, along with several biographies of the Colonel and the one book that he wrote."

"General Custer," she corrected.

He grinned. "That was a brevet promotion, given during the Civil War for outstanding courage under fire. His actual military rank was Colonel, at the time he died."

"You read about him, too?" she asked.

He nodded. "These were some of the first books I was exposed to as a child. My mother was big on reading skills," he said coolly. "Her picks were nonfiction, mostly chemistry and physics. Grandmother's were more palatable."

She noted the play of emotions on his lean, hard face. "Your mother was a scientist," she said suddenly, and wondered where the memory came from.

"Yes." He stared at her intently. "A research chemist. She died when we were young."

"You didn't like her very much, did you?"

"I hated her," he said flatly. "She made my grandmother miserable, making fun of her reading tastes, the way she dressed, her skills as a homemaker. She demeaned her."

"Was your grandmother your mother's mother?"

He shook his head. "My father's mother. In her day, she was an elegant horsewoman. She won trophies. And she was an actress before she married. But that, to my mother's mind, was fluff. She only admired women with Mensa-level IQs and science degrees."

"What about your father, couldn't he stop her from tormenting the old lady?"

He scoffed. "He was never here. He was too involved with making money to pay much attention to what went on around the house."

Her eyes narrowed. "You must have had an interesting childhood."

He cocked an eyebrow. "There's a Chinese curse—'may you live in interesting times.' That would have been appropriate for it."

She didn't quite know what to say. He looked so alone. "Nell said she died in a tornado. Your grandmother, I mean."

He nodded. "She was trying to save her horse. She'd had him for twenty-five years, ridden him in competition. She loved him more than any other thing here, except maybe me." He grimaced. "I'll never forget watching them bring her down from the treetop. She looked like a broken doll." His eyes closed briefly. "I don't have much luck with women, when it comes to love."

That was a curious thing to say. She felt odd as he said it, as if she knew something more about that, but couldn't quite call it up.

"I guess life is a connected series of hard knocks," she mused.

He glanced at her. "Your own life hasn't been any bed of roses," he commented. "You lost your father when you were born, and your grandfather and your mother only six months apart."

"Did I?" she wondered.

He cursed under his breath. "I shouldn't have said that."

"It didn't trigger any memories," she assured him, managing a smile. "I'm pretty blank about recent events. Well, I remember I'm graduating," she amended, "and that I borrowed Marge's car to drive to your house . . ." She hesitated. "Marge's car . . ."

"Stop trying to force it," he said, tapping her knee with a hard finger. "Your memory will come back when it's ready to."

"Nell said she was quitting. Did you have a row with her?"

"Did she say that I had?" he asked warily.

"She didn't say much of anything, J.B.," she muttered. "I can't get a straight answer out of anybody, even that nice man who was in the emergency room with me." She hesitated. "Has he come by to see me?"

He shifted restlessly. "Why ask me?" he wondered, but he wouldn't meet her eyes.

"He did come to see me!" she exclaimed, seeing the truth in the ruddy color that ran along his high cheek-bones. "He came, and you wouldn't let him in!"

Eight

J.B. not only looked angry, he looked frustrated. "Coltrain said you didn't need visitors for two or three days, at least," he said firmly.

She was still staring at him, with wide pale green eyes. "But why not? Grange won't tell me anything. Every time I asked a question, he pretended to be deaf." Her eyes narrowed. "Just like you, J.B.," she added.

He patted her knee. "We're all trying to spare you any unnecessary pain," he said.

"So you're admitting that it would be painful if I remembered why you and I argued," she said.

He glared. "Life is mostly painful," he pointed out. "You and I have had disagreements before."

"Have we? And you seem like a man with such a sunny, even disposition," she said innocently.

"Ha!" came an unexpected comment from the hall.

They both turned to the doorway, and there stood Nell, in a housecoat with her hair in curlers, glaring at both of them.

"I have an even disposition," he argued.

"Evenly bad," Nell agreed. "She should be asleep," she said, nodding at Tellie.

He got to his feet. "So she should." He took the book away from Tellie and put it on the bedside table. "Go to sleep."

"Can I get you anything before I go to bed, Tellie?" Nell asked.

"No, but thanks."

J.B. pulled the pillows out from under her back and eased her down on the bed. He pulled up the covers, studied her amusedly and suddenly bent and brushed his hard mouth over her forehead. "Sleep tight, little bit." He turned off the lamp.

"I don't need tucking in," she said.

"It never hurts," he mused. He passed Nell. "You going to stand there all night? She needs her sleep."

"You're the one who was keeping her awake!" Nell muttered.

"I was not . . . !"

Their voices, harsh and curt, came through the closed door after he'd pulled it shut. Tellie sighed and closed her eyes. What an odd pair.

The next morning, there was heavy rain and lightning. Thunder shook the house. Alarmed, Tellie turned on the weather alert console next to her bed and listened to the forecast. There was a tornado watch for Jacobs County, among others in south Texas.

She grimaced, remembering tornadoes in the past. She'd seen one go through when she was a little girl. It hadn't touched down near their house, but she could never forget the color of the clouds that contained it. They were a neon-green, like slimy pond algae, enclosed in thick gray swirls. She got to her feet, a little shakily, and went to the window to look out. The clouds were dark and thick and lightning struck down out of them so unexpectedly, and violently, that she jumped.

"Get away from that window!" J.B. snapped from the doorway.

She turned, her heart racing from the double impact of the storm and his temper. "I was just looking," she protested.

He closed the door behind him, striding toward her with single-minded determination. He swung her up in his powerful arms and carried her back to bed.

"Lightning strikes the highest point. There are no trees taller than the house. Get the point?" he asked.

She clung to his strong neck, savoring his strength. "I get it."

He eased her down on the pillow, his green eyes staring straight into hers as he rested his hands beside her head on the bed. "How's your head?"

"Still there," she mused. "It does throb a bit."

"No wonder," he said. He searched her eyes for so long that her heart raced. He looked down at her pajama jacket and his teeth clenched. She looked down, too, but she didn't see anything that would make him frown.

"What's wrong?" she asked.

He drew in a long breath. "You're still a child, Tellie," he said, more for his own benefit than for hers. He stood up. "Ready for breakfast?"

She frowned. "Why did you say that?"

He stuck his hands in his pockets and went to the window to look out.

"You'll get struck by lightning," she chided, throwing his own accusation back at him.

"I won't."

His back was arrow straight. She stared at it longingly. It had been sweet to lie in his arms while he carried her. She felt an odd stirring deep in her belly.

"You really hate storms, don't you?" she said.

"Most people do, if they've ever lived through one."

She remembered what he'd told her about the grandmother he loved so much, and how she'd died in a tornado. "I've only seen one up close."

He turned toward her, his eyes watchful and quiet.

"What are you thinking?" she asked.

"I don't remember you going out on more than two dates the whole time you were in high school."

The reference to the past, luckily, went right over her head. She blinked. "I was always shy around boys," she confessed. "And none of them really appealed to me. Especially not the jocks. I hate sports."

He laughed softly. "Was that why?"

She twisted the hem of the sheet between her fingers and stared at them. "You must have noticed at some point that I'm not overly brainy or especially beautiful."

He frowned. "What does that have to do with dating?"

"Everything, in high school," she reminded him

curtly. "Besides all that, most boys these days want girls who don't mind giving out. I did. It got around after I poured a cup of hot chocolate all over Barry Cramer when he slid his hand under my skirt at a party."

"He did what?" he exclaimed, eyes flaming.

The rush to anger surprised her. He'd never shown any particular emotion about her infrequent dates.

"I told him that a hamburger and a movie didn't entitle him to that sort of perk."

"You should have told me," he said curtly. "I'd have decked him!"

Her cheeks colored faintly. "That would have got around, too, and I'd never have had another date."

He moved close to the bed and studied her like an insect on a pin. "I don't suppose you'd have encouraged a boy to touch you like that."

"Whatever for?" she asked curiously.

His jaw clenched, hard. "Tellie, don't you . . . feel anything . . . with boys?"

She cocked her head. "Like what?"

"Like an urge to kiss them, to let them touch you."

The color in her cheeks mushroomed. She could barely meet his eyes. "I don't . . . I don't feel that way."

"Ever?"

She shifted, frowning. "What's gotten into you, J.B.? I'm only seventeen. There's plenty of time for that kind of thing when I'm old enough to think about marriage."

His fist clenched in his pocket. Even at her real age, he'd never seen her get flustered around anything male, not even himself. The one time he'd kissed her with intent, on his own sofa, she'd given in at once, but she'd been reticent and shocked more than aroused. He was beginning to think that she'd never been aroused in her life; not even with him. It stung his pride, in one way, and made him hungry in another. It disturbed him that he couldn't make Tellie want him. God knew, most other women did.

"Is that what you meant, when you called me a kid earlier?" she asked seriously.

He moved to the foot of the bed, with his hands still shoved deep in his pockets, and stared at her. "Yes. That's what I meant. You're completely unawakened. In this modern day and age, it's almost unthinkable for a woman your age to know so little about men."

"Well, gee whiz, I guess I'd better rush right out there and get myself a prescription for the pill and get busy, huh?" she asked rakishly. "Heaven forbid that I should be a throwback to a more conservative age, especially in this house! Didn't you write the book on sexual liberation?"

He felt uncomfortable. "Running with the crowd is the coward's way out. You have to have the courage of your convictions."

"You've just told me to forget them and follow the example of the Romans."

He glowered. "I did not!"

She threw up her hands. "Then why are you complaining?"

"I wasn't complaining!"

"You don't have to yell at me," she muttered. "I'm sick."

"I think I'm going to be," he said under his breath.

"You sure have changed since I was in the wreck," she murmured, staring at him curiously. "I never thought I'd see the day when you'd advise me to go out and get experienced with men. I don't even know any men." She frowned. "Well, that's not completely true. I know Grange." Her eyes brightened. "Maybe I can ask him to give me some pointers. He looks like he's been around!"

J.B. looked more and more like the storm outside. He moved toward the bed and sat down beside her, leaning down with his hands on either side of her face on the pillow. "You don't need lessons from Grange," he said through his teeth. "When you're ready to learn," he added on a deep, husky breath, "I'll teach you."

Ripples of pleasure ran up and down her nerves, leaving chill bumps of excitement all over her arms. Her breath caught at the thought of J.B.'s hard, beautiful mouth on her lips.

His eyes went down to her pajama jacket, and this time they lingered. For an instant, he looked shocked. Then his eyes began to glitter and he smiled, very slowly.

She looked down again, too, but she couldn't see anything unusual. Well, her nipples were tight and hard, and a little uncomfortable. That was because of her sudden chill. Wasn't it?

Her eyes met his again, with a faint question in them.

"You don't even understand this, do you?" he asked, and suddenly, without warning, he drew the tip of his forefinger right over one distended nipple with the faintest soft brushing motion.

She gasped out loud and her body arched. She looked, and was, shocked out of her mind.

J.B.'s green eyes darkened with sudden hunger. His gaze fell to her parted, full lips, to the pulse throbbing in the hollow of her throat. He ached to open her pajama top and put his mouth right on her breast. Unthinkable pleasures were burning in the back of his mind.

Tellie was frightened, both of what was happening to her body, and of letting him know how vulnerable she was. There was something vaguely unsettling about the way he was looking at her. It brought back a twinge of memory, of J.B. mocking her because she was weak toward him . . .

She brought up her arms and crossed them over her breasts.

"Spoilsport," he murmured, meeting her shocked eyes.

She fought to breathe normally. "J. B. Hammock, I'm seventeen years old!" she burst out.

He started to contradict her and realized at once that he didn't dare. He scowled and got to his feet abruptly. What the hell was he thinking?

He ran a hand over his hair and turned away. "I've got to go to town and see a Realtor about a parcel of land that's just come up for sale," he said in a strangely thick tone. "It adjoins my north pasture. I'll send Nell up with breakfast."

"Yes, that would be . . . that would be nice."

He glanced back at her from the door. He felt frustrated and guilty. But behind all that, he was elated. Tellie was vulnerable to him, and not just in the girlish way she had been for the past few years. She was vulnerable as a woman. It was the first time her body had reacted to his touch in that particular way.

He should have been ashamed of himself. He wasn't. His eyes slid over her body in the pajamas as if she belonged to him already. He couldn't hide the pride of possession that he felt.

It made Tellie shake inside. Surely he wasn't thinking . . . ?

"Don't beat yourself to death over it," he said. "We're all human, Tellie. Even me. See you later."

He went out quickly and closed the door behind him, before his aching body could provoke him into even worse indiscretions than he'd already committed.

Nell brought breakfast and stared worriedly at Tellie's high color. "You're not having a relapse, are you?" she asked, worried.

Tellie wished she could confide in the housekeeper, or in someone. But she had no close friends, and she couldn't even have told Marge. She couldn't talk to Marge about her brother!

"Nothing's wrong, honest," Tellie said. "I went to look out the window, and a big flash of lightning almost made me jump out of my skin. I'm still reeling."

Nell's face relaxed. "Is that all?" She smiled. "I don't mind storms, but J.B. is always uneasy. Don't forget his grandmother died in a tornado outbreak."

"He told me," she said.

"Did he, now?" Nell exclaimed. "He doesn't talk about the old lady much."

Tellie nodded. "He doesn't talk about much of anything personal," she agreed. She frowned. "I wonder if he confides in his fashion dolls?"

Nell didn't get the point at first, but when she did, she burst out laughing. "That was mean, Tellie."

Tellie just grinned. She was going to forget what J.B. had done in those few tempestuous seconds. She was certain that he'd regretted it.

Sure enough, he didn't come in to see her at all the rest of the day. Next morning, he went out without a word.

About lunchtime, Grange showed up. Since J.B. wasn't there to keep him out, Nell escorted him up to Tellie's room with a conspiratorial grin.

"Company," Nell announced. "He can stay for lunch. I'll bring up a double tray." She went out, but left the door open.

Grange moved toward the bed with his wide-brimmed hat in his hand. He'd had a haircut and a close shave. He smelled nice, very masculine. His dark eyes twinkled as he studied Tellie in her pink pajamas.

She felt self-conscious and pulled the sheet up higher.

He laughed. "Sorry."

She shrugged. "I'm not used to men seeing me in my nightclothes," she told him. It wasn't totally true. He didn't know, and J.B. seemed to constantly forget, that she'd been almost assaulted by a boy in her early teens. It hadn't left immense scars, but she still felt uneasy about her body. She wasn't comfortable with men. She wondered if she should admit that to J.B. It might soften his provocative attitude toward her.

"I'll try not to stare," Grange promised, smiling as he sat down in the chair beside her bed. "How are you feeling?"

"Much better," she said. "I wanted to get up, but Nell won't let me."

"Concussion is tricky," he replied, and he didn't smile. "The first few days are chancy. Better you stay put in bed, just for the time being."

She smiled at him. "I'll bet you've seen your share of injuries, being in the military."

He nodded. "Concussion isn't all that uncommon in war. I've seen some nasty head injuries that looked pretty innocent at first. Better safe than sorry."

"I hate being confined," she confessed. "I want to get out and do things, but Dr. Coltrain said I couldn't. Nell and J.B. are worse than jailers," she added.

He chuckled. "Nell's a character." He hesitated. "Did you know there's a chef in the kitchen, complete with tall white hat and French accent?"

She nodded. "That's Albert," she replied. "He's been here for the past ten years. J.B. likes continental cuisine."

"He seems to be intimidated by Nell," he observed.

"He probably is. Gossip is that when Albert came here, Nell was in possession of the kitchen and unwilling to turn it over to a foreigner. They say," she added in a soft, conspiratorial tone, "that she chased him into the living room with a rolling pin when he refused to make dumplings her way. It took a pay raise and a color television for his room to keep him here. J.B. and Nell had a real falling out about that, and she threatened to quit. She got a raise, too." She laughed shortly. She'd remembered something from the past! Surely the rest couldn't be far behind now.

Grange chuckled at what she'd told him about Nell. "She seems formidable enough."

"She is. She and J.B. argue most of the time, but it's usually in a good-natured way."

He put his hat on the floor beside his chair and raked a hand through his neatly trimmed straight dark hair. "When they let you out of here, we'll go take in a new science-fiction movie. How about that?"

She smiled. "Sounds like fun." She was curious about him. He didn't seem the sort of man to be vulnerable to women, but it was apparent that he liked Tellie. "Do you have family here in Jacobsville?" she asked in all innocence.

His face hardened. His dark eyes narrowed. "No."

She frowned. She'd struck a nerve. "I'm sorry, is there something else I don't remember—?"

"There's a lot," he cut her off, but gently. "You're bound to wander into a few thickets before you find the right path. Don't worry about it."

She drew in a long breath. "I feel like I'm walking around in a fog. Everybody's hiding things from me."

"It's necessary. Just for a week or so," he promised.

"You know about me, don't you? Can't you tell me?"

He held up a hand and laughed. "I'd just as soon not get on the wrong side of Hammock while you're living under his roof. I'd lose visiting privileges. I may lose them anyway, if Nell spills the beans that I've been here while he was out."

"Doesn't he like you?"

"He doesn't like most people," he agreed. "Especially me, at the moment."

"What did you do to him?"

"It's a long story, and it doesn't concern you right now," he said quietly.

She flushed. His voice had been very curt.

"Don't look like that," he said, feeling guilty "I don't want to hurt you. J.B. and I have an unfortunate history, that's all."

She blinked. "It sounds unpleasant."

"It was," he confessed. "But it happened a long time ago. Right now, our only concern is to get you well again."

Footsteps sounded on the staircase and a minute later, Nell walked in with a tray holding two plates, two glasses of iced tea and a vase full of yellow roses.

"Never thought I'd get up the stairs with everything intact," she laughed as Grange got up and took the tray from her, setting it down gently on the mahogany side table by the bed.

"The roses," Tellie exclaimed. "They're beautiful!"

"Glad you like them," Grange said easily, and with a smile. "We do live in Texas, after all."

" 'The Yellow Rose of Texas,' " she recalled the song. She reached over and plucked one of the stems out of the vase to smell it. There was a delicate, sweet scent. "I don't think I've ever had a bouquet of flowers in my life," she added, confused.

"You haven't," Nell replied for her. She sounded irritated. "Nice of Grange to remember that sick people usually like flowers."

She smiled at him. "Wasn't it?" she laughed. "I'll enjoy them. Thank you."

"My pleasure," he replied, and his voice was soft.

Nell stuck a plate in his hands and then put Tellie's on her lap. "Eat, before the bread molds," she told them. "That's homemade chicken salad, and I put up those dill pickles myself last summer."

"Looks delicious," Grange said. "You didn't have to do this, Nell."

"I enjoy making a few things on my own," she said. She grimaced. "I had to lock Albert in the closet, of course. His idea of a sandwich involves shrimp and sauce and a lettuce leaf on a single piece of toasted rye bread." She looked disgusted.

"That's not my idea of one," Grange had to admit.

"This is really good," Tellie exclaimed after she bit into her sandwich.

"Yes, it is," Grange seconded. "I didn't have time for breakfast this morning."

138

"Enjoy," Nell said, smiling. "I'll be back up for the tray later."

They both nodded, too involved with chewing to answer.

Grange entertained her with stories from his childhood. She loved the one about the cowboy, notorious for his incredible nicotine habit, who drove his employer's Land Rover out into the desert on a drunken joyride, forgetting to take along a shovel or bottled water or even a flashlight. He ran out of gas halfway back and when they found him the next morning, almost dead of dehydration, the first thing he asked for was a cigarette.

"What happened to him?" she asked, laughing.

"After he got over the experience, the boss put him on permanent barn duty, cleaning out the horse stalls. The cowboy couldn't get a job anywhere else locally because of that smoking habit, so he was pretty much stuck."

"He couldn't quit?"

"He wouldn't quit," he elaborated. "Then he met this waitress and fell head over heels for her. He quit smoking, stopped drinking and married her. He owns a ranch of his own now and they've got two kids." His dark eyes twinkled. "Just goes to show that the love of a good woman can save a bad man."

She pursed her lips. "I'll keep that in mind."

He laughed. "I'm not a bad man," he pointed out. "I just have a few rough edges and a problem with authority figures."

"Is that why you don't get along with J.B.?"

He shook his head. "That's because we're too much alike in temperament," he said. He checked his watch. "I've got to run," he said, swooping up his hat as he got to his feet. "Can't afford to tick off my boss!"

"Will you come again?" she asked.

"The minute the coast is clear," he promised, laughing. "If Nell doesn't sell us out."

"She won't. She's furious at J.B. I don't know why, nobody tells me anything, but I overheard her say that she'd quit and had to come back to take care of me. Apparently she and J.B. had a major blowup before I got hurt. I wish I knew why."

"One of these days, I'm sure you'll find out. Keep getting better."

"I'll do my best. Thanks again. For the roses, and for coming to see me."

"I enjoyed it. Thanks for lunch."

She grinned. "I'll cook next time."

"Something to look forward to," he teased, winking at her.

J.B. came in late. Apparently he'd been out with whichever girlfriend he was dating, because he was dressed up and a faint hint of perfume clung to his shirt as he sat down in the chair beside Tellie's bed. But he looked more worried than weary, and he wasn't smiling.

She eyed him warily. "Is something wrong?" she asked.

140

He leaned back in the chair, one long leg crossed over the other. She noted how shiny his hand-tooled black boots were, how well his slacks fit those powerful legs. She shook herself mentally. She didn't need to notice such things about him.

"Nothing much," he said. Actually he was worried about Marge. She was in the early stages of treatment for high blood pressure, and she'd had a bad dizzy spell this afternoon. The girls had called him at work, and he'd gone right over. He'd phoned Coltrain, only to be reassured that some dizziness was most likely a side effect of the drug. She was having a hard time coping, and she missed Tellie, as well as being worried about her health. J.B. had assured Marge that Tellie was going to be fine, but his sister wanted to see Tellie. He couldn't manage that. Not yet.

He drew in a long breath, wondering how to avoid the subject. That was when he looked at her bedside table carelessly and saw the huge bouquet of yellow roses. His green eyes began to glitter as he stared at her.

"And just where," he asked with soft fury, "did you get a bouquet of roses?"

Nine

"They were a present," Tellie said quickly.

"Were they?" he asked curtly. "From whom?"

She didn't want to say it. There was going to be a terrible explosion when she admitted that she'd had a visitor. It didn't take mind-reading skills to realize that J.B. didn't like Grange.

She swallowed. "Grange brought them to me."

The green eyes were really glittering now. "When?"

"He stopped by on his lunch hour," she said. She glared up at him. "Listen, there's nothing wrong with having company when you're sick!"

"You're in your damned pajamas!" he shot back.

"So?" she asked belligerently. "You're looking at me in them, aren't you?"

"I don't count."

"Oh. I see." She didn't, but it was best not to argue with a madman, which is how he looked at the moment.

His lips made a thin line. "I'm family."

She might have believed that before yesterday, she thought, when he'd touched her so intimately.

The memory colored her cheeks. He saw it, and a slow, possessive smile tugged up his firm, chiseled lips. That made the blush worse.

"You don't think of me as family?" he asked softly.

She wanted to dive under the covers. It wasn't fair that he could reduce her to this sort of mindless hunger.

He leaned over her, the anger gone, replaced by open curiosity and something else, less definable.

His fingers speared through her dark hair, holding her head inches from the pillow behind her. His chest rose and fell quickly, like her own. His free hand went to her soft mouth and traced lazily around the upper lip, and then the lower one, with a sensuality that made her feel extremely odd.

"I'm . . . seventeen," she choked, grasping for a way to save herself.

His dark green gaze fell to her parted lips. "You're not," he said huskily, and the hand in her hair contracted. "It can't hurt for you to know your real age. You're almost twenty-two. Fair game," he added under his breath, and all at once his hard, sensuous mouth came down on her lips with firm purpose.

She gasped in surprise, and her hand went to his chest. That was a mistake, because it was unbuttoned in front and her fingers were enmeshed in thick, curling dark hair that covered the powerful muscles.

His head lifted, as if the contact affected him. His eyes narrowed. His heart, under her fingertips, beat strongly and a little fast.

"You shouldn't . . ." she began, frightened of what was happening to her.

"I've waited a long time for this," he said enigmatically. He bent to her mouth again. "There's nothing to be afraid of, Tellie," he whispered into her lips. "Nothing at all . . ."

The pressure increased little by little. Her fingers dug into his chest as odd sensations worked themselves down her body, and she shivered.

He smiled against her parted lips. "It's about time," he murmured, and his mouth grew insistent.

She felt his body slowly move closer, so that they were lying breast to breast on the soft mattress. One lean hand slid under the pajama top, against her rib cage, warm and teasing. She should grab his wrist and stop him, her mind was saying, because this wasn't right. He was a notorious womanizer and she was like his ward. She was far too young to be exposed to such experienced ardor. She was . . . but he'd said she was almost twenty-two years old. Why hadn't she remembered her age?

His hand contracted in her soft hair. "Stop thinking," he bit off against her mouth. "Kiss me, Tellie," he breathed, and his hand suddenly moved up and cupped her soft, firm breast. His head lifted, to watch her stunned, delighted reaction.

For an instant, she stiffened. But then his thumb rubbed tenderly over the swollen nipple, and a ripple of ardent desire raged in her veins. She drew in a shivery, shaking breath. The pressure increased, just enough to be arousing. She arched involuntarily, and moaned.

"Yes," he said, as though she'd spoken.

His hand swallowed her whole, and his mouth moved gently onto her parted lips, teasing, exploring, demanding. All her defenses were down. There was no tomorrow. She had J.B. in her arms, wanting her. Whether it was wrong or not, she couldn't resist him. She'd never known that her body could experience anything so passionately satisfying. She felt swollen. She wanted to pull him closer. She wanted to touch him, as he was touching her. She wanted . . . everything!

Her arms slid up around his neck and she arched into the warm pressure of his hand on her body.

His mouth increased its pressure, until he broke open her mouth and his tongue moved inside, in slow, insistent thrusts that made her moan loudly. She'd never been kissed in such an intimate way. She'd never wanted to be. But this was delicious. It was the most delicious taste of a man she'd ever had. She wanted more.

He hadn't meant to let things get so far out of control, but he went under just as quickly as she did. His hand left her breast to flick open the buttons of her pajama jacket. She whispered something, but he didn't hear it. He was blind, deaf, dumb to anything except the taste and feel of her innocence.

He kissed her again, ardently, and while she followed his mouth, he stripped her out of the pajama top and opened the rest of the buttons over his broad chest. He gathered her hungrily to him, dragging his chest against hers so that the rasp of hair only accentuated the pleasure she was feeling.

When his lean, hard body moved over hers, she was beyond any sort of protest. Her long legs parted eagerly to admit the intimacy of his body. She shivered when she felt him against her. She hadn't realized how it would feel, when a man was aroused, although she'd read enough about it in her life. Other women were vocal about their own affairs, and Tellie had learned from listening to them talk. She'd been sure that she would never be vulnerable to a man like this, that she'd never be tempted to give in with no thought beyond satisfaction. What she was feeling now put the lie to her overconfidence. She was as helpless as any woman in love.

Even knowing that J.B. was involved more with his body than his mind didn't help her resist him. Whatever he wanted, he could have. She just didn't want him to stop. She was drowning in sensation, pulsating with the sweetest, sharpest hunger she'd ever known.

"I've waited so long, Tellie," he groaned into her mouth. His hand went under her hips and lifted her closer into a much more intimate position that made her shudder all over. "God, baby, I'm on fire!"

So was she, but she couldn't manage words. She arched up toward him, barely aware that he was looking down at her bare breasts. He bent and put his mouth on them, savoring their firm softness, their eager response to his ardor.

Her nails bit into his shoulders. She rocked with him, feeling the slow spiral of satisfaction that was just beginning, like a flash of light that obliterated reason, thought, hope. She only wanted him never to stop.

His lean hand went to the snap that held her pajama bottoms in place, just as loud footsteps sounded on the staircase, accompanied by muttering that was all too familiar.

J.B. lifted his head. He looked as shocked as Tellie felt. He looked down at her breasts and ruddy color flamed over his high cheekbones. Then he looked toward the hall and realized belatedly that the door was standing wide open.

With a furious curse, he moved away from her and got to his feet, slinging the cover over her only a minute before Nell walked in with a tray. Luckily for both of them, she was too concerned over not dumping milk and cookies all over the floor to notice how flushed they were.

J.B. had time to fasten his shirt. Tellie had the sheet up to her neck, covering the open pajama jacket she'd pulled on.

"Thought you might like a snack," Nell said, smiling as she put the tray down next to the vase of roses.

"I would. Thanks, Nell," Tellie said in an oddly husky tone.

J.B. kept his back to Nell as he went toward the door. "I've got a phone call to make. Sleep tight, Tellie."

"You, too, J.B.," she said, amazed at her acting ability, and his.

When he was gone, Nell moved the roses a little farther onto the table. "Aren't they beautiful, though?" she asked Tellie as she sniffed them. "Grange has good taste."

"Yes, he does," Tellie said, forcing a smile.

Nell glanced at her curiously. "You look very flushed. You're not running a fever, are you?" she asked worriedly.

Tellie bit her lower lip and tasted J.B. there. She looked at Nell innocently. "J.B. and I had words," she lied.

Nell frowned. "Over what?"

"The roses," Tellie replied. "He didn't like the idea that Grange was here."

Nell sighed, falling for the ruse. "I was afraid he wouldn't."

"Do you know why he dislikes him so much?" Tellie asked. "I mean, he agreed that I could go out with Grange, apparently. It seems odd that he wouldn't have stopped me."

"He couldn't," Nell said. "After all, you're of age . . ." She stopped and put her hand over her mouth, looking guilty.

"I'm almost twenty-two," Tellie said, avoiding Nell's gaze. "I . . . remembered."

"Well, that's progress!"

It wasn't, but Tellie wasn't about to admit to Nell that she'd had a heavy petting session with J.B. in her own bed and learned about her age that way. She could still hardly believe what had happened. If Nell hadn't walked up the staircase just at that moment . . . It didn't bear thinking about. What had she done? She knew J.B. was a womanizer. He didn't love women; she knew that even though she couldn't remember why. She'd given him liberties that he wasn't entitled to. Why?

"You look tired," Nell said. "Drink up that milk and eat those cookies. Leave the tray. I'll get it in the morning. Can I bring you anything else?"

A good psychiatrist, Tellie thought, but didn't dare say. She smiled. "No. Thanks a lot, Nell."

"You're very welcome. Sleep well."

She'd never sleep again, she imagined. "You, too."

The door closed behind her. Tellie sat up and started to rebutton her jacket. Her breasts had faint marks on them from J.B.'s insistent mouth. She looked at them and got aroused all over again. What was happening? She knew, she just knew, that J.B. had never touched her like that before. Why had he done it?

She lay awake long into the night, worrying the question.

The next morning, Nell told her that J.B. had suddenly had to fly to a meeting in Las Vegas, a cattlemen's seminar of some sort.

Tellie wasn't really surprised. Perhaps J.B. was a little embarrassed, as she was, about what they'd done together.

"He didn't take his girlfriend with him, either," Nell said. "That's so strange. He takes her everywhere else."

Tellie felt her heart stop beating. "His girlfriend?" she prompted.

"Sorry. I keep forgetting that your memory's limping. Bella," she added. "She's a beauty contestant. J.B.'s been dating her for several weeks."

Tellie stared at her hands. "Is he serious about her?"

"He's never serious about women," Nell replied. "But that doesn't mean he won't have them around. Bella travels with him, mostly, and she spends the occasional weekend in the guest room."

"This room?" Tellie asked, horrified, looking around her.

"No, of course not," Nell said, not noticing Tellie's look of horror. "She stays in that frilly pink room that we usually put women guests in. Looks like a fashion-doll box inside," she added with a chuckle. "You'd be as out of place there as I would."

The implication made her uneasy. J.B. was intimate with the beauty contestant, if she was spending weekends with him. The pain rippled down her spine as she considered how easily she'd given in to him the night before. He was used to women falling all over him, wasn't he? And Tellie wasn't immune. She wasn't even respected, or he'd never have touched her when she was a guest in his house. The more she thought about it, the angrier she got. He was involved with another woman, and making passes at Tellie. What was wrong with him?

On the other hand, what was wrong with her? She only wished she knew.

She got out of bed and started helping Nell around the house, despite her protests.

"I can't stay in bed my whole life, Nell," Tellie argued. "I'll never get better that way."

"I suppose not," the older woman admitted. "But you do have to take it easy."

"I will." She pushed the lightweight electric broom into the living room. The sofa caught her attention again, as it had when she'd come home from the hospital. She moved to its back and ran her hand over the smooth cloth fabric, frowning. Why did this sofa make her uneasy? What had happened in this room in the past that upset her?

She turned to Nell. "What did J.B. and I argue about?" she asked.

Nell stopped dead and stared. She was obviously hesitating while she tried to find an answer that would be safe.

"Was it over a woman?" Tellie persisted.

Nell didn't reply, but she flushed.

So that was it, Tellie thought. She must have been jealous of the mysterious Bella and said something to J.B. that hit him wrong. But, why would she have been jealous? She was almost certain that J.B. had never touched her intimately in their past.

"Honey, don't try so hard to remember," Nell cautioned. "Enjoy these few days and don't try to think about the past."

"Was it bad?" she wondered aloud.

Nell grimaced. "In a way, yes, it was," she replied. "But I can't tell you any more. I'll get in trouble. It might damage you, to know too much too soon. Dr. Coltrain was very specific."

Tellie gnawed her lower lip. "I've already graduated from high school, haven't I?" she asked.

Nell nodded, reluctantly.

"Do I have a job?"

"You had a summer job, at the Ballenger Brothers feedlot. That's where you met Grange."

She felt a twinge of memory trying to come back. There was something between J.B. and Grange, something about a woman. Not the beauty contestant, but some other woman. There was a painful secret . . .

She caught her head and held it, feeling it throb.

Nell moved forward and took her by the shoulders.

151

"Stop trying to force the memories," she cautioned. "Take it one day at a time. Right now, let's do some vacuuming. Then we'll make a cake. You can invite Grange over to supper, if you like," she added, inspired. "J.B. won't be around to protest."

Tellie smiled. "I'd enjoy that."

"So would I. We'll call him at the feedlot, when we're through cleaning."

"Okay."

They did the necessary housekeeping and then made a huge chocolate pound cake. Grange was enthusiastic about coming for a meal, and Tellie was surprised at the warm feeling he evoked in her. It was friendly, though, not the tempestuous surging of her heart that she felt when she remembered the touch of J.B.'s hard lips on her mouth.

She had a suitcase that she didn't remember packing. Inside was a pretty pink striped dress. She wore that, and light makeup, for the meal. Grange showed up on time, wearing a sports jacket with dress slacks, a white shirt and a tie. He paid for dressing. He was very good-looking.

"You look nice," Tellie told him warmly as he followed her into the dining room, where the table was already set.

"So do you," he replied, producing another bouquet of flowers from behind his back, and presenting them with a grin.

"Thanks!" she exclaimed. "You shouldn't have!"

"You love flowers," he said. "I didn't think you had enough."

She gave him a wary look. "Is that the whole truth?" she asked suspiciously and with a mischievous grin, "or did you think you'd irritate J.B. if I had more flowers in my room?"

He chuckled. "Can't put anything past you, can I?" he asked.

"Thanks anyway," she told him. "I'll just put them in water. Sit down! Nell and I chased Albert out of the kitchen and did everything ourselves. I understand he's down at the goldfish pond slitting his wrists . . ."

"He is not!" Nell exclaimed. "You stop that!"

Tellie grinned. "Sorry. Couldn't resist it. He seems to think he owns the kitchen."

"Well, he doesn't," Nell said. "Not until I leave for good."

Leave. Leave. Tellie frowned, staring into space. Nell had quit. Tellie had been crying. Nell was shouting. J.B. was shouting back. It was raining . . .

Grange caught her as she fell and carried her into the living room. He put her down on the sofa. Nell ran for a wet cloth.

Tellie groaned as she opened her eyes. "I remembered an argument," she said huskily. "You and J.B. were yelling at each other . . ."

Nell frowned. "You couldn't have heard us," she said. "You'd already run out the door, into the rain."

Tellie could see the road, blinded by rain, feel the tires giving way, feel the car going into the ditch . . . !

She gasped. "I wrecked the car. I saw it!"

Nell sat down beside her and put an arm around her. "Grange saved you," she told the younger woman. "He came along in time to stop you from drowning. The ditch the car went into was full of water."

Tellie held the cloth to her forehead. She swallowed, and then swallowed again. There were odd, disturbing flashes. J.B.'s furious face. A blond woman, staring at her. There were harsh words, but she couldn't remember what they were. She didn't want to remember!

"Did I thank you for saving me?" she asked Grange, trying to ward off the memories.

He smiled worriedly. "Of course you did. How do you feel now?"

"Silly," she said sheepishly as she sat up. "I'm sorry. There were some really odd flashbacks. I don't understand them at all."

"Don't try to," Nell said firmly. "Come on in here and eat. Let time take care of the rest."

She got up, holding on to Grange's arm for support. She drew in a long, slow breath. "One way and another, it's been a rough few days," she said.

"You don't know the half," Nell said under her breath, but she didn't let Tellie hear her.

The next day was Saturday. Tellie went out to the barn to see the sick calf that was being kept there while it was being treated. In another stall was a huge, black stallion. He didn't like company. He pawed and snorted as Tellie walked past him. He was J.B.'s. She knew, without remembering or being told. She moved to another stall, where a beautiful Palomino mare was eating from a feed trough. The horse perked up when she saw Tellie, and left her food to come to the front of the stall and nose Tellie's outstretched hand.

"Sand," Tellie murmured. She laughed. "That's your name. Sand! J.B. lets me ride you!"

The horse nudged her hand again. She smoothed the white blaze between the mare's eyes lazily. She was beginning to recover some memories. The rest, she was sure, would come in time.

She wandered past the goldfish pond on the patio and stared down at the pretty red and gold and white fish swimming around water lilies and lotus plants. The facade was stacked yellow bricks, and there were huge flat limestone slabs all around it, making an endless seat for people to watch the fish. There were small trees nearby and a white wrought-iron furniture set with a patio umbrella. In fair weather, it must be heavenly to sit there. She heard a car drive up and wondered who it was. Not J.B., she was sure. It was too soon for him to be back. Monday, Nell said, was the earliest they could expect him. Perhaps it was one of the cowboys.

It was a dreary day, not good exploring weather. She wondered how Marge and the girls were, and wanted to see them. She dreaded seeing J.B. again. Things had changed between them. She was uneasy when she considered that J.B. had left town so quickly afterward, as if his conscience bothered him. Or was it that he was afraid Tellie would start thinking about something serious? She knew so little about relationships . . .

She walked back through the side door into the living room and stopped suddenly. There was a beautiful blond woman standing in the doorway. She was wearing a yellow dress that fit her like a second skin. She had long, wavy, beautiful hair and a perfectly made-up face. She was svelte and sophisticated, and she was giving Tellie a look that could have boiled water.

"So you're the reason I've had to be kept away from the house," the woman said haughtily.

That blonde was familiar, Tellie thought suddenly, and she wanted to run. She didn't want to talk to this person, to be around her. She was a threat.

The woman sensed Tellie's discomfort and smiled coldly. "Don't tell me you've forgotten me?" she drawled. "Not after you walked right in and interrupted me and J.B. on that very sofa?"

Sofa. J.B. Two people in the sofa, both half-naked. J.B. furious and yelling. Nell rushing to see why Tellie was crying.

Tellie put her hands to her mouth as the memories began to rush at her, like daggers. It was all coming back. J.B. had called her ugly. A stray. He could never love her. He didn't want her. He'd said that!

There was more. He'd missed her graduation from college and lied about it. He'd had his secretary buy Tellie a graduation present—he hadn't even cared enough to do it himself. He'd accused Tellie of panting after him like a pet dog. He'd said he was sick of her . . . pawing him . . . trying to touch him.

She felt the rise of nausea in her throat like a living thing. She brushed past the blonde and ran for the hall bathroom, slamming the door behind her. She barely made it to the sink before she lost her breakfast.

"Tellie?"

The door opened. Nell came in, worried. "Are you all right? Oh, for goodness sake . . . !"

She grabbed a washcloth from the linen closet and wet it, bathing Tellie's white face. "Come on. Let's get you back to bed."

"That woman . . ." Tellie choked.

"I showed her the door," Nell said coldly. "She won't come back in a hurry, I guarantee!"

"But I recognized her," Tellie said unsteadily. "She and J.B. were on the sofa together, half-naked. He yelled at me. He accused me of trying to paw him. He said he was sick of the way I followed him around. He said . . ." She swallowed the pain. "He said I was nothing but an ugly stray that he'd taken in, and that he could never want me." Tears rolled down her cheek. "He said he never . . . wanted to see me again!"

"Tellie," Nell began miserably, not knowing what to say.

"Why did he bring me here, after that?" she asked tearfully.

"He felt guilty," Nell said gently. "It was his fault that

you wrecked the car. You would have died, if Grange hadn't found you."

Tellie wiped her eyes with the wet washcloth. "I knew there was something," she choked. "Some reason that he wasn't giving me. Guilt. Just guilt." Was that why he'd kissed her so hungrily, too? Was he trying to make amends for what he'd said? But it was only the truth. He didn't want her. He found her repulsive . . .

The tears poured down her face. She wanted to climb into a hole. That beautiful blonde was J.B.'s woman. She'd come to Marge's house with J.B., and she'd insulted Tellie. They'd argued, and J.B. had shown Tellie what a hold he had over her, using her weakness for him as a punishment. She closed her eyes. How could he have treated her so horribly?

"I want to go back to Marge's house," Tellie said shakily. "Before he comes home." She looked into Nell's eyes. "And then I never want to see him again, as long as I live!"

Ten

Nell couldn't talk Tellie into staying at the house, not even when she assured her that J.B. wouldn't be back until Monday. Tellie had remembered that Marge had a heart attack, and she was frantic until Nell assured her that Marge was going to be all right. It was even lucky that they'd found the high blood pressure before it killed her.

Now that Tellie remembered everything, there were

no more barriers to her going to Marge. She remembered her job at the feedlot, as well, and hoped she still had it. But she phoned Justin at home and he assured her that her job would be waiting when she was recovered. That was a load off her mind.

She didn't dare think about J.B. It was too terrible, remembering the hurtful things he'd said to her. She knew she'd never forgive him for the way he'd reacted when she'd tried to tell him about Marge, much less for his ardor when he knew there was no future in it. He'd taunted her with her feelings one time too many. She wondered what sort of cruel game he'd been playing in her bedroom at his house.

Marge and the girls met her at the door, hugging her warmly. Nell had driven her there, and she was carrying two suitcases.

"Are you sure about this?" Nell asked worriedly.

Marge nodded, smiling warmly. "You know you're welcome here. None of us will yell at you, and we'll all be grateful that we don't have to depend on Dawn's cooking for . . ."

"Mother!" Dawn exclaimed.

"Sorry," Marge said, hugging her daughter. "I love you, baby, but you know you're terrible in the kitchen, even if you can sing like an angel. Nobody's perfect."

"J.B. thinks he is," Nell muttered.

Marge laughed. "Not anymore, I'll bet. I hope you left him a note, at least."

"I did," Nell confessed. "Brief, and to the point. I

hope that blond fashion doll of his can cook and clean."

"That isn't likely," Tellie said coolly. "But they can always get takeout."

"Are you sure you're okay?" Marge asked Tellie, moving to hug her, too. "Your color's bad."

"So is yours, worrywart," Tellie said with warm affection, returning the hug. "But I reckon the two of us will manage somehow, with a little help."

"Between us," Marge sighed, "we barely make one well person."

"I'll fatten you both up with healthy, nonsalty fare," Nell promised. "Dawn and Brandi can see me to my room and help me unpack. Right?"

The girls grinned. "You bet!" they chorused, delighted to see the end of meal preparation and house-work. Nell was the best in town at housekeeping.

They marched up the staircase together, the girls helping with the luggage.

Marge studied Tellie closely, her sharp eyes missing nothing. "You wouldn't be here unless something major had happened. What was it?"

"My memory came back," Tellie said, perching on the arm of the sofa.

"Did it have any help?" the older woman asked shrewdly.

Tellie grimaced, her eyes lowering to the sea-blue carpet. "Bella kindly filled me in on a few things."

Marge cursed under her breath as forcefully as J.B. ever had. "That woman is a menace!" she raged. "Copper Coltrain said it would be dangerous for us to

160

force-feed you facts about the past until you remembered them naturally!"

"I'm sure she only wanted J.B. to herself again, and thought she was helping him get me out of the way. I don't mind," Tellie added at once. "J.B. raised hell when Grange came and brought me roses. At least you're not likely to mind that."

Marge smiled. "No, I'm not. I like your friend Grange."

Tellie's eyes were sad and wise. "He's been a wonderful friend. Who'd have thought he'd turn out to be pleasant company, with his background?"

"Not anyone locally, that's for sure." Marge sat down on the sofa, too. She was still pale. "Nothing wrong," she assured Tellie, who was watching her closely. "The medicine still makes me a little dizzy, but it's perfectly natural. Otherwise, I'm seeing an improvement all around. I think it's going to work."

"Goodness, I hope so," Tellie said gently. She smiled. "We can't lose you."

"You aren't going to. Nice of you to bring Nell with you," she added wryly. "Housework and cooking was really getting to us, without you here. Did she come willingly?"

"She met me at the front door with her suitcase," she replied. "She was furious at what Bella had done. She thinks maybe J.B. put her up to it."

Marge scowled. "That isn't likely. Whatever his faults, J.B. has a big heart. He was really concerned about you."

"He felt guilty," Tellie translated, "because he felt responsible for the wreck. He yelled at me and said some terrible things," she added, without elaborating. Her sad eyes were evidence enough of the pain he'd caused Tellie. "I couldn't stay under his roof, when I remembered them."

Marge picked at a fingernail. "That bad?"

Tellie nodded, averting her eyes.

"Then I suppose it's just as well for you to stay here."

"I don't want to see him," she told Marge. "Not ever again. He's had one too many free shots at me. I'll finish out the week at Ballenger's when I get back on my feet, and then I'm going to ask my alma mater for an adjunct position teaching history for night students. I can teach at night and go to classes during the day. The semester starts very soon."

"Is it wise, to run away from a problem?" the other woman queried.

"In this case, it's the better part of valor," she replied grimly. "J.B. didn't just say unpleasant things to me, Marge, he actually taunted me with the way I felt about him. That's hitting below the belt, even for J.B."

"He did that?" Marge exclaimed.

"Yes. And that's why I'm leaving." She got up. She smiled at Marge. "Not to worry, you'll have Nell to take over here for me, and pamper all three of you. I won't have to be nervous about leaving you. Nell will make sure you do what the doctor says, and she'll cook healthy meals for you."

"J.B. is going to be furious when he gets home and finds you both gone," Marge predicted. She was glad she wasn't going to have to be the one to tell him.

It was dark and raining when J.B. climbed out of the limo he'd hired to take him to and from the airport. He signed the charge slip, tipped the driver with two big bills and carried his flight bag and attaché case up the driveway to the house.

It was oddly quiet when he used his key to open the front door. Usually there was a television going in Nell's room, which could be heard faintly coming down the staircase. There were no lights on upstairs, and no smells of cooking.

He frowned. Odd, that. He put down his suitcase and attaché case, and opened the living room door.

Bella was stretched out on the sofa wearing a pink gown and negligee and a come-hither smile.

"Welcome home, darling," she purred. "I knew you wouldn't mind if I moved into my old room."

He was worn-out and half out of humor. Bella's mood didn't help. What in the world must Tellie be thinking of this new development, despite her lack of memory.

"What did you tell Tellie?" he asked.

Her eyebrows arched. "I only reminded her of how she found us together the night your sister had to go to the hospital," she drawled. "She remembered every-thing else just fine, after that, and she went to your sister's." She smiled seductively. "We've got the

163

whole night to ourselves! I'm cooking TV dinners. They'll be ready in about ten minutes. Then we can have champagne and go to bed . . ."

"You told her that?" he burst out, horrified.

She glowered, moving to sit up. "Now, J.B., you know she was getting on your nerves. You never go to those stupid seminars, you just wanted to get away from her."

"That isn't true," he shot back. And it wasn't. He'd gone to give Tellie, and himself, breathing space. Her ardent response had left his head spinning. For the first time in their relationship, Tellie had responded to him as a woman would, with passion and hunger. He hadn't slept an entire night since, reliving the delicious interlude time after time. He'd had to leave, to make sure he didn't press Tellie too hard when she was fragile, make sure he didn't force memories she wasn't ready for. He'd hoped to have time to show her how tender he could be, before she remembered how cruel he'd been. Now the chance was gone forever, and the source of his failure was sprawled on his sofa in a negligee planning to replace Tellie. He felt a surge of pure revulsion as he looked at Bella.

"Nell!" he called loudly.

"Oh, she went with the girl to your sister's," Bella said, yawning. "She left a note on your desk."

He went to his study to retrieve it, feeling cold and dead inside. The note was scribbled on a memo pad. It just said that Nell was going to work for Marge, and that she hoped Bella was domesticated.

He threw it down on the desk, overwhelmed with frustration. Bella came up behind him and slid her arms around him.

"I'll check on the TV dinners," she whispered. "Then we can have some fun . . ."

He jerked away from her, his green eyes blazing. "Get dressed and go home," he said shortly. He took out his wallet and stuffed some bills into her hand.

"Where are you going?" she exclaimed when he walked toward the front door.

"To get Nell and Tellie back," he said shortly, and kept walking.

Bella actually screamed. But it didn't do any good. He didn't even turn his head.

Marge met him at the door. She didn't invite him in.

"I'm sorry," she said, stepping onto the porch with him. "But Tellie's been through enough today. She doesn't want to see you."

He shoved his hands into his pockets, staring at her. "I leave town for two days and the world caves in on me," he bit off.

"You can thank yourself for that," his sister replied. Her dark eyes narrowed. "Was it necessary to use Tellie's weakness for you against her like a weapon?"

He paled a little. "She told you?" he asked slowly.

"The bare bones, nothing more. It was low, J.B., even for you. Just lately, you're someone I don't know."

His broad shoulders lifted and fell. "Grange brought back some painful memories."

"Tellie wasn't responsible for them," she reminded him bluntly.

He drew in a sharp breath. "She won't give up Grange. It's disloyal."

"They're friends. Not that you'd recognize the reference. You don't have friends, J.B., you have hot dates," she pointed out. "Albert phoned and said your current heartthrob was preparing dinner for you. Frozen dinners, I believe . . . ?"

"I didn't ask Bella to move in while I was away!" he shot back. "And I sure as hell didn't authorize her to fill Tellie in on the past!"

"I'm sure she thought she was doing you a favor, and removing the opposition at the same time," Marge said, folding her arms across her chest. "I love you, J.B., but I'm your sister and I can afford to. You're hard on women, especially on Tellie. Lately it's like you're punishing her for having feelings for you."

His high cheekbones went ruddy. He looked away from Marge. "I didn't want anything permanent, at first."

"Then you should never have encouraged Tellie, in any way."

He sighed roughly. He couldn't explain. It flattered him, softened him, that Tellie thought the world revolved around him. She made him feel special, just by caring for him. But she hadn't been able to give him passion, and he was afraid to take a chance on her without it. For years, he'd given up passionate love, he was afraid of it. When Tellie left for college he didn't

166

want her to be hurt, but he didn't want to be hurt himself. He loved too deeply, too intensely. He couldn't live with losing another woman, the way he'd lost his late fiancée. But now Tellie was a woman, and he felt differently. How was he going to explain that to Tellie if he couldn't get near her?

"Tellie's changed in the past few weeks. So have I." He shifted. "It's hard to put it into words."

Marge knew that he had a difficult time talking about feelings. She and J.B. weren't twins, but they'd always been close. She moved toward him and put a gentle hand on his arm. "Tellie's going back to Houston in a week," she said quietly. "Do her a favor, and leave her alone while she finishes out her notice at the feedlot. Let her get used to being herself. Then maybe you can talk to her, and she'll listen. She's just hurt, J.B."

"She wasn't going back to school until fall semester," he said shortly. "She's been through a lot. She shouldn't start putting pressure on herself this soon."

"She doesn't see it that way. She's going to teach adult education at her college at night and attend classes during the day during summer semester." She lowered her eyes to his chest. "I want her to be happy. She's never going to be able to cope with the future until you're out of her life. I know you're fond of her, J.B., but it would be kinder to let her go."

He knew that. But he couldn't let her go, now that he knew what he wanted. He couldn't! His face reflected his inner struggle.

Her hand closed hard on his forearm. "Listen to me,"

she said firmly, "you of all people should know how painful it is to love someone you can't have. Everyone knows you don't want marriage or children, you just want a good time. Bella's your sort of woman. You couldn't hurt her if you hit her in the head with a brickbat, she's so thick. Just enjoy what you've got, J.B., and let Tellie heal."

He met her eyes. His were turbulent with frustrated need and worry. "I wanted to try to make it up to her," he bit off.

"Make what up to her?"

He looked away. "So much," he said absently. "I've never given her anything except pain, but I want to make her happy."

"You can't do that," his sister said quietly. "Not unless you want her for keeps."

His eyes narrowed in pain. He *did* want her for keeps. But he was afraid.

"Don't try to make her into a casual lover," Marge cautioned. "You'd destroy her."

"Don't you think I know?" he asked curtly. He turned away. "Maybe you're right, Marge," he said finally, defeated. "It would be kinder to let go for the time being. It's just that she cared for me, and I gave her nothing but mockery and indifference."

"You can't help that. You can't love people just because they want you to," Marge said wisely. "Tellie's going to make some lucky man a wonderful wife," she added gently. "She'll be the best mother a child could want. Don't rob her of that potential by giving her false hope."

Tellie, with a child. The anguish he felt was shocking. Tellie, married to another man, having children with another man, growing old with another man. He'd never considered the possibility that Tellie could turn her affections to someone else. He'd assumed that she'd always worship him. He'd given her the best reason on earth to hate him, by mocking her love for him.

"I've been taking a long look at myself," he said quietly. "I didn't like what I saw. I've been so busy protecting myself from pain that I've inflicted it on Tellie continuously. I didn't mean to. It was self-defense."

"It was cruel," Marge agreed. "Throwing Bella up to her, parading the woman here in Tellie's home, taunting her for wanting to take care of you." She shook her head. "I'm amazed that she was strong enough to take it all these years. I couldn't have."

"What about Grange?" he asked bitterly.

"What about him?" she replied. "She's very fond of him, and vice versa. But he isn't really in the running right now. He's a man with a past, a rebel who isn't comfortable in domestic surroundings. He likes having someone to take to the movies, but he's years away from being comfortable with even the idea of marriage."

That made J.B. feel somewhat better. Not a lot. He was thinking how miserable Tellie must be, having been force-fed the most horrible memories of her recent life. Coltrain said that her mind had been hiding from the trauma of the past. He didn't know that J.B. was responsible for it. He kept seeing Tellie on the gurney as she came into the emergency room, bruised and bleeding, and unconscious. If Grange hadn't shown up, Tellie would have drowned. He'd have had two dead women on his conscience, when one had always been too many.

The thought of Tellie, dead, was nauseating. She'd looked up to him since her early teens, followed him around, ached to just have him look at her. He'd denigrated those tender feelings and made her look like a lovesick fool. That, too, had been frustration, because he wanted a woman's passion from Tellie and she hadn't been able to give it to him. Not until now. He was sorry he'd been cruel to her in his anguish. But he couldn't go back and do it over again. He had to find some way back to Tellie. Some way to make up for what he'd done to her. Some way to convince her that he wanted a future with her.

"Tell her that I'm sorry," he said through his teeth. "She won't believe it, I know, but tell her anyway."

"Sorry for what?"

He met her eyes. "For everything."

"She'll be all right," Marge told him. "Really she will. She's stronger than I ever imagined."

"She's had so little love in her life," he recalled bitterly. "Her mother didn't really care much for her. She lost her grandfather at the time she needed him most. I shoved her off onto you and took it for granted that she'd spend her life looking up to me like some sort of hero." He drew in a long breath. "She was assaulted,

170

you know, when she was fourteen. I've pushed that to the back of my mind and neither of us insisted that she go on with therapy after a few short sessions. Maybe those memories had her on the rack, and she couldn't even talk about them."

Marge chuckled. "Think so? Tellie beat the stuffing out of the little creep and testified against him, as well. He never even got to touch her inappropriately. No, she's over that, honestly."

"Even if she is, I made her suffer for having the gall to develop a crush on me."

He sounded disgusted with himself. Marge could have told him that it was no crush that lasted for years and years and took all sorts of punishment for the privilege of idolizing him. But he probably knew already.

He looked up at the darkening sky. "I know how it must look, that I've had Bella staying at the house, and taken her on trips with me. But I've never slept with her," he added with brutal honesty.

Marge's eyebrows arched. That was an odd admission, from a rounder like her brother. "It can't be from lack of encouragement," she pointed out.

"No," he agreed. "It couldn't."

She felt inadequate to the task at hand. She wondered if she was doing the right thing by asking him not to approach Tellie. But she didn't really know what else there was to do. She felt sorry for both of them, especially for her brother who'd apparently discovered feelings for Tellie too late.

"I don't want a wife right now," he said, but without

the old conviction. "She knows that, anyway."

"Sure she does," his sister agreed.

He turned and looked down at her with soft affection. "You doing okay?"

She nodded, smiling. "Nell's going to be a treasure. I can't do a lot of the stuff I used to, and the girls hate cooking and housework. With Tellie gone, it's up to us to manage. Nell will make my life so much easier. I can probably even go back to work when the medicine takes hold."

"Do you want to?" he asked curiously.

"Yes," she said. "I'm not the sort of person who enjoys staying at home with nothing intellectually challenging to do. I'd at least like to work on committees or help with community projects. Money isn't enough. Happiness takes more than a padded bank account."

"I'm finding that out," J.B. agreed, smiling. "You take care of yourself. If you need me, I'm just at the other end of the phone."

"I know that. I love you," she said, hugging him warmly.

He cleared his throat. "Yeah. Me, too." Expressing emotion was hard for him. She knew it.

She pulled away. "Go home and eat your frozen dinner."

He grimaced. "I sent Bella home in a cab. It's probably carbon by now."

"Albert will fix you something."

"When he finds out why Tellie's gone, I wouldn't bet on having anything edible in the near future."

"There are good restaurants all over Jacobsville," she pointed out.

He laughed good-naturedly. "I suppose I'll find one. Take care."

"You, too. Good night."

She closed the door and went back inside. Tellie's light was off when she went upstairs. The younger woman was probably worn completely out from the day's turmoil. She wished Tellie had never spent any time with J.B. at all. Maybe then she'd have been spared so much heartache.

Tellie was hard at work on her last day at the feedlot. It was a sweltering hot Friday, and storm clouds were gathering on the horizon. The wind was moving at a clip fast enough to stand the state flag out from its flagpole. When she went to lunch, sand blew right into her face as she climbed into Marge's car to drive home and eat.

The wind pushed the little car all over the road. It wasn't raining yet, but it looked as if it might rain buckets full.

She turned on the radio. There was a weather bulletin, noting that a tornado watch was in effect for Jacobsville and surrounding counties until late that afternoon. Tellie was afraid of tornadoes. She hoped she never had to contend with one as long as she lived.

She ate a quick lunch, surrounded by Marge and Nell and the girls, since it was a teacher workday and they weren't in school. But when she was ready to leave, the skies were suddenly jet-black and the wind was roaring like a lion outside.

"Don't you dare get in that car," Marge threatened.

"Look at the color of those clouds," Nell added, looking past them out the door.

The clouds were a neon-green, and there was a strange shape growing in them, emphasized by the increasing volume and force of the wind.

While they stood on the porch with the doors open, the sound of a siren broke into the dull rumble of thunder.

"Is that an ambulance?" Dawn asked curiously.

"No," Nell said at once. "It's the tornado alert, it's the siren on top of the courthouse." She ran for the weather radio, and found it ringing its batteries off. There was a steady red light on the console. Even before it blared out the words *tornado warning,* Nell knew what was coming.

"We have to get into the basement, right now!" Nell said, rushing to the hall staircase. "Come on!"

They piled after her, down the carpeted stairs and into the basement, into the room that had been especially built in case of tornadoes. It was steel-reinforced, with battery-powered lights and radio, water, provisions and spare batteries. The wind was audible even down there, now.

They closed themselves into the sheltered room and sat down on the carpeted floor to wait it out. Nell turned on the battery-powered scanner and instead of the weather, she turned to the fire and police frequencies.

Sharp orders in deep voices heralded the first of the damage. One fire and rescue unit was already on its way out Caldwell Road from a report of a trailer being demolished. There came other reports, one after another. A roof was off this building, a barn collapsed, there were trees down in the road, trees down on power lines, trees falling on cars. It was the worst damage Tellie had heard about in her young life.

She thought about J.B., alone in his house with memories of his grandmother dying in such a storm. She wished she could stop caring about what happened to him. She couldn't. He was too much a part of her life, regardless of the treatment he'd handed out to her.

"I hope J.B.'s all right," Tellie murmured as the overhead light flickered and went out on the heels of a violent burst of thunder.

"So do I," Marge replied. "But he's got a shelter of his own. I'm sure he's in it."

The violence outside escalated. Tellie hid her head in her crossed arms and prayed that nobody would be killed.

Several minutes later, Nell eased the door open and listened for a minute before she went up the staircase. She was back shortly.

"It's over," she called to the others. "There's a little thunder, but it's far away, and you can see some blue sky. There are two big oak trees down in the front yard, though."

"I hope nobody got hurt," Marge mumbled as they

went up the staircase.

"Call the house," Tellie pleaded with Nell. "Make sure J.B.'s all right."

Nell grimaced, but she did it. Argue they might, but she was fond of her old boss. The others stared at Nell while she listened. She winced and put down the receiver with a sad face.

"The lines are down," she said worriedly.

"We could drive over there and see," Dawn suggested.

Tellie recalled painfully the last time she'd driven over to J.B.'s place to tell him about a disaster. She couldn't bear to do it again.

"We can't get out of the driveway," Marge said uneasily. "One of the oaks is blocking the whole driveway."

"Give me your cell phone," Nell told Marge. "I'll call my cousin at the police department and get him to have someone check."

The joy of small-town life, Tellie was thinking. Surely the police could find out for them if J.B. was safe. Tellie prayed silently while Nell waited for her cousin to come to the phone.

She listened, spoke into the phone, and then listened again, grimacing. She thanked her cousin and put down the phone, facing the others with obvious reluctance.

"The tornado hit J.B.'s house and took off the corner where his office was. He's been taken to the hospital. My cousin doesn't know how bad he's hurt. There were some fatalities," she added, wincing when she saw their faces go white. Arguments and disagreements aside, J.B. was precious to everyone in the room.

Tellie spoke for all of them. "I'm going to the hospital," she said, "if I have to walk the whole five miles!"

Eleven

As it happened, they managed to get around the tree in their raincoats and walk out to the main highway. It was still raining, but the storm was over. Marge got on her cell phone and called her friend Barbara, who phoned one of the local firemen, an off-duty officer who agreed to pick them up and take them to the hospital.

When they got there, J.B. was in the emergency room sitting on an examination table, grinning. He had a cut across his forehead and a bruise on his bare shoulder, but his spirit seemed perfectly unstoppable.

Tellie almost ran to him. Almost. But just as she tensed to do it, a blond head came into view under J.B.'s other arm. Bella, in tears, sobbing, as she clung to J.B.'s bare chest mumbling how happy she was that he wasn't badly hurt.

She drew back and Marge and Nell and the girls joined her, out of sight of J.B. and Bella.

"You go ahead," she told them. "But . . . don't tell him I was here. Okay?"

Marge nodded, the others agreed. They understood without a word of explanation. "Go on out front, honey," Marge said gently. "We'll find you there when we're through."

"Okay. Thanks," Tellie said huskily, with a forced smile. Her heart was breaking all over again.

As Marge and the girls moved into the cubicle, Tellie walked back to the front entrance where there were chairs and a sofa around the information desk. She couldn't bring herself to walk into that room. J.B. hadn't looked as if he disliked Bella, despite what Marge had told her about his anger that Bella had spilled the beans about Tellie's past. He looked amazingly content, and his arm had been firm and close around Bella's shoulders.

Why, Tellie asked herself, did she continually bash her stupid head against brick walls? Love was such a painful emotion. Someday, she promised herself, she was going to learn how to turn it off. At least, as far as J. B. Hammock was concerned!

She didn't see Bella walk past the waiting room. She hardly looked up until Marge and the girls came back.

"He's going to be all right," Marge told her, hugging her gently. "Just a few cuts and bruises, nothing else. Let's go home."

Tellie smiled back, but only with her eyes.

J.B. buttoned his shirt while Bella stood waiting with his tie. He felt empty. Tellie hadn't even bothered to come and see about him. Nothing in recent years had hurt so much. She'd finally given up on him for good.

"We can get Albert to fix you something nice for breakfast," Bella said brightly.

"I'm not hungry." He took the tie and put it in place.

"At least Marge and the girls cared enough to brave the storm to see me. Tellie couldn't be bothered, I guess," he said bitterly.

"She was in the waiting room," Bella said blankly.

He scowled. "Doing what?"

Bella shrugged one thin shoulder. "Crying."

Crying. She'd come to see about him after all, but she hadn't come into the room? Then he remembered that when Marge and the girls came in, he had Bella in his arms. He winced mentally. No wonder Tellie had taken off like that. She thought . . .

He looked down at Bella shrewdly. "I'm going to have to let Albert go," he said with calculated sadness. "With all the damage the storm did to the house and barn, I'm going to go in the hole for sure. It's been a bad year for cattle ranchers anyway."

Bella was very still. "You mean, you might lose everything?"

He nodded. "Well, I don't mind hard work. It's a challenge to start from scratch. You can move in with me, Bella, and take over the housekeeping and cooking . . ."

"I, uh, I have an invitation from my aunt in the Bahamas to come stay the summer with her," Bella said at once. "I'm really sorry, J.B., but I'm not the pioneering type, and I hate housework." She smiled. "It was fun while it lasted."

"Yes," he said, hiding a smile. "It was."

The next day was taken up finding insurance adjusters

and contractors to repair the damage at the ranch. He'd lost several head of livestock to injuries from falling trees and flying debris. The barn would have to be rebuilt, and the front part of the house would need some repair, as well. He wasn't worried, though. He could well afford what needed doing. He smiled at his subterfuge with Bella. As he'd suspected, she'd only wanted him for as long as she thought he was rich and could take her to five-star restaurants and buy her expensive presents.

When he had the repairs in hand, he put on a gray vested business suit, polished boots and his best creamy Stetson, and went over to Marge's to have a showdown with Tellie.

Nell opened the door, her eyes guilty and welcoming all at once. "Glad you're okay, boss," she said stiffly.

"Me, too," he agreed. "Where is everybody?"

"In the kitchen. We're just having lunch. There's plenty," she added.

He slipped an arm around her shoulders and kissed her wrinkled forehead with genuine affection. "I've missed you," he said simply, and walked her into the kitchen.

Marge and the girls looked up, smiling happily. They all rushed to hug him and fuss over him.

"Nell made minestrone," Marge said. "Sit down and have a bowl with us."

"It smells delicious," he remarked, putting his hat on the counter. He sat down, looking around curiously. "Where's Tellie?"

There was a long silence. Marge put down her spoon. "She's gone."

"Gone?" he exclaimed. "Where?"

"To Houston," Marge replied sadly. "She phoned some classmates and found an apartment she could share, then she phoned the dean at home and arranged to teach as an adjunct for night classes. Orientation was today, so she was able to sign up for her master's classes."

J.B. looked at his bowl with blind eyes. Tellie had gone away. She'd seen him with Bella, decided that he didn't want her, cut her losses and run for the border. Added to what she'd remembered, the painful things he'd said to her the day of the wreck, he couldn't blame her for that. She didn't know how drastically he'd changed toward her. Now he'd have to find a way back into her life. It wasn't going to be easy. She'd never fully trust him again.

But he wasn't giving up before he'd started, he told himself firmly. He'd never really tried to court Tellie. If she still cared at all, she wouldn't be able to resist him—any more than he could resist her.

Tellie was finding her new routine wearing. She taught a night class in history for four hours, two nights a week, and she went to classes three other days during the week. She was young and strong, and she knew she could cope. But she didn't sleep well, remembering Bella curled close in J.B.'s arm the night of the tornado. He wouldn't marry the beautiful woman, she knew that. He wouldn't marry anyone. But he had nothing to offer Tellie, and she knew, and suffered for it.

One of her classmates, John, who'd helped her find a room the night before she came back to Houston, paused by her table in the college coffeehouse.

"Tellie, can you cover for me in anthropology?" he asked. "I've got to work tomorrow morning."

She grinned up at him. John, like her, was doing master's work, although his was in anthropology. Tellie was taking the course as an elective. "I'll make sure I take good notes. How about covering for me in literature? I'll have a test to grade in my night school course."

"No problem," he said. He grinned down at her, with a hand on the back of her chair. "Sure you don't want to go out to dinner with me Friday night?"

He was good-looking, and sweet, but he liked to drink and Tellie didn't. She was searching for a reply when she turned her gaze to the door.

Her heart jumped up into her throat. J.B. was standing just inside the door of the crowded café, searching. He spotted her and came right on, his eyes never leaving her as he wound through the crowd.

He stopped at her table. He spared John a brief glance that made veiled threats.

"I'd better run," John said abruptly. "See you later, Tellie."

"Sure thing."

J.B. pulled out a chair and sat down, tossing his hat idly onto the chair beside hers. He didn't smile. His eyes were intent, curiously warm.

"You ran, Tellie."

She couldn't pretend not to know what he was talking about. She pushed back her wavy hair and picked up her coffee cup. "It seemed sensible."

"Did it?"

She sipped coffee. "Did the tornado do much damage at the ranch?"

He shrugged. "Enough to keep me busy for several days, or I'd have been here sooner," he told her. He paused as the waitress came by, to order himself a cup of cappuccino. He glanced at Tellie and grinned. "Make that two cups," he told the waitress. She smiled and went to fill the order, while J.B. watched Tellie's face. "You can't afford it on your budget," he said knowingly. "My treat."

"Thanks," she murmured.

He leaned back in his chair and looked at her, intently, unsmiling. "Heard from Grange?"

She shook her head. "He phoned before I left Jacobsville to say he was going back to Washington, D.C. Apparently he was subpoenaed to testify against his former commanding officer, who's being court-martialed."

He nodded. "Cag Hart told me. He and Blake Kemp and Grange served in the same division in Iraq. He said Grange's commanding officer had him thrown out of the army and took credit for a successful incursion that was Grange's idea."

"He told me," she replied.

The waitress came back with steaming cappuccino for both of them. J.B. picked his up and sipped it. Tellie sniffed hers with her eyes closed, smiling. She loved the rich brew.

After a minute J.B. met her eyes again. "Tellie, is this what you really want?" he asked, indicating the coffee-house and the college campus.

The question startled her. She toyed with the handle of her cup. "Of course it is," she lied. "When I get my doctorate, I can teach at college level."

"And that's all you want from life?" he asked. "A career?"

She couldn't look at him. "We both know I'll never get very far any other way. I have plenty of friends who cry on my shoulder about their girlfriends or ask me to take notes for them in class, or keep their cats when they go on holiday." She shrugged. "I'm not the sort of woman that men want for keeps."

He closed his eyes on a wave of guilt. He'd said such horrible things to her. She already had a low self-image. He'd lowered it more, in a fit of bad temper.

"Beauty alone isn't worth much," he said after a minute. "Neither is wealth. After I got out of the emergency room, I went home to an empty house, Tellie," he said sadly. "I stood there in the vestibule, with crystal chandeliers and Italian marble all around me, mahogany staircases, Persian rugs . . . and suddenly it felt like being alone in a tomb. You know what, Tellie? Wealth isn't enough. In fact, it's nothing, unless you have someone to share it with."

"You've got Bella," she said with more bitterness than she knew.

He laughed. "I told her I was in the hole and likely to lose everything," he commented amusedly. "She suddenly remembered an invitation to spend the summer in the sun with her aunt."

Tellie's eyes lifted to his. She was afraid to hope.

He reached across the table and curled her fingers into his. "Finish your cappuccino," he said gently. "I want to talk to you."

She was hardly aware of what she was doing. This must be a dream, J.B. sitting here with her, holding her hand. She was going to wake up any minute. Meanwhile, she might as well enjoy the fantasy. She smiled at him and sipped her cappuccino.

He took her out to his car and put her in the passenger side. When he was seated behind the wheel, he reached back and brought out a shopping bag with colored paper tastefully arranged in it. "Open it," he said.

She reached in and pulled out a beautiful lacy black mantilla with red roses embroidered across it. She caught her breath. She collected the beautiful things. This was the prettiest one she'd ever seen. She looked at him with a question in her eyes.

"I picked it out myself," he told her quietly. "I didn't send Jarrett shopping this time. Don't stop. There's more, in the bottom of the bag."

Puzzled, she reached down and her fingers closed around a velvety box with a bow on it. She pulled it out and stared at it curiously. Another watch? she wondered.

"Go on. Open it."

She took off the bow and opened the box. Inside was . . . another box. Frowning, she opened that one, too, and found a very small square box. She opened that one, too, and caught her breath. It was a diamond. Not too big, not too small, but of perfect quality in what looked like expensive yellow gold. Next to it was an equally elegant band studded with diamonds that matched the solitaire.

J.B. was holding his breath, although it didn't show.

She met his searching gaze. "I . . . don't understand."

He took the box from her, lifted out the solitaire and slid it gently onto her ring finger. "Now, do you understand?"

She was afraid to try. Surely it was still part of the dream. If not, it was a cruel joke.

"You don't want me," she said bitterly. "I'm ugly, and you can't bear me to touch you . . . !"

He pulled her across into his arms and kissed her with unabashed passion, cradling her against his broad chest while his mouth proceeded to wear down all her protests. When she was clinging to him, breathless, he folded her in his arms and rocked her hungrily.

"I was ashamed that you found me like that with Bella," he said through his teeth. "It was like getting caught red-handed in an adulterous relationship. For God's sake, don't you have any idea how I feel about you, Tellie?" he groaned. "I was frustrated and impatient, and Bella was handy. But I've never slept with her," he added firmly. "And I never would have. You have to believe that."

She was reeling mentally. She let her head slide back on his shoulder so that she could see his face. "But . . . why were you so cruel . . . ?"

His lean hand pressed against her cheek caressingly. "Do you remember when you were eighteen?" he asked huskily. "And I made love to you on the couch in the living room?"

She flushed. "Yes."

"You loved being kissed. But when I started touching you, I felt you draw back. You liked kissing me, but you weren't comfortable with anything more intimate than that. You didn't feel anything approaching passion, Tellie. You were like a child." He sucked in a harsh breath. "And I was burning, aching, to have you. I knew you were too young. It was unfair of me to push you into a relationship you weren't nearly ready for." He studied her shocked face. "So I drew back and waited. And waited. I grew bitter from the waiting. It made me cruel."

Her eyes were wide, shocked, delighted, as she realized what had been going on. She hadn't dreamed that he might feel something this powerful for her, and for so long.

"Yes, now you see it, don't you?" he breathed, lowering his mouth to hers again, savoring its shy response. "I was at the end of my rope, and you seemed just the same. Desperation made me cruel.

Then," he whispered, "you lost your memory and I had you in my house. I touched you . . . and you wanted me." He kissed her hungrily, roughly. "I was over the moon, Tellie. You'd forgotten, temporarily, all the terrible things I said to you when you caught me with Bella. But it ended, all too soon. Your memory came back." He buried his face in her neck, rocking her. "You hated me. I didn't know what to do. So I waited some more. And hoped. I might still be waiting, except that Bella told me she saw you crying in the emergency room when I thought you hadn't even come to see about me after the tornado hit." He kissed her again, hungrily, and felt with a sense of wonder her arms clinging to him, her mouth answering the passion of his own.

"You brought that awful woman to Marge's house and let her insult me," she complained hotly.

He kissed her, laughing. "You were jealous," he replied, unashamedly happy. "It gave me hope. I dangled Bella to make you jealous. It worked almost too well."

"You vicious man," she accused, but she was smiling.

"Look who's talking," he chided. "Grange gave me some bad moments."

"I like him very much, but I didn't love him," she replied quietly.

"No. You love me," he whispered. His eyes ate her face. "And I love you, Tellie," he whispered as he bent again to her mouth. "I love you with all my heart!"

She closed her eyes and gave in to his ardor, blind to

the fact that they were sitting in a parked car on a college campus.

She felt some disturbance around her and looked up. In front of the car were three students with quickly printed squares of poster paper. One said "9," and two said "10." They were grading J.B. on his technique. He followed her amused gaze and burst out laughing.

He drew her up closer. "Don't protest," he murmured as his head bent. "I'm going for a perfect score . . ."

He took her back to his hotel. His intentions were honorable, of course, but it was inevitable that once they were alone, he'd kiss her. He did, and all at once the raging fever he'd contained for so many years broke its bonds with glorious abandon.

"J.B.," she protested weakly as he picked her up and carried her into one of the bedrooms in his suite, closing the door firmly behind them.

"You can't stop an avalanche, honey," he ground out against her mouth. "I'm sorry. I love you. I can't wait any longer . . . !"

She was flat on her back, her jeans on the floor, swiftly joined by her blouse and everything underneath. He looked down at her with a harsh, heartfelt groan. "I knew you'd be perfect, Tellie," he whispered as he bent to touch his mouth reverently to her breasts.

There was hardly any sane answer to that sort of rapt delight. She felt faintly apprehensive, but she was wearing an engagement ring and it was apparent that it wasn't a sham, or a dream. She came straight up off the bed as his mouth increased its warm pressure on her breast and began to taste it with his tongue.

"Like that, do you?" he whispered huskily. "It's only the beginning."

As he spoke, he sat up and quickly removed every bit of fabric that would have separated them.

Shyly she looked at his hard, muscular body with eyes that showed equal parts of awe and apprehension.

"People have been doing this for millennia," he whispered as he lowered his body against hers. "If it didn't feel good, nobody would indulge."

"Well, yes, but . . ." she began.

His lean hand smoothed over her belly. "You have to trust me," he said softly. "I won't hurt you. I swear it."

Her body relaxed a little. "I've heard stories," she began.

"I'm not in them," he replied easily, smiling. "If I were less modest, I'd tell you that women used to write my telephone number on bathroom walls."

That tickled her and she laughed. "Don't you dare brag about your conquests," she muttered.

He laughed. "Practice," he said against her mouth. "I was practicing, while I waited for you. And this is what I learned, Tellie," he added as his body slid against hers.

She felt his hands and his mouth all over her. The lights were on and she couldn't have cared less. Sensation upon sensation rippled through her untried body. She saw J.B.'s face harden, his dark green eyes glitter as he increased the pressure of his powerful legs to part hers, as his mouth swallowed one small, firm breast and drew his tongue against it in a sweet, harsh rhythm.

He was touching her in ways she'd only read about. She gasped and moaned and, finally, begged. She hadn't dreamed that her body could feel such things, could react in this headlong, demanding, insistent way to a man's slow, insistent ardor.

The slow thrust of his body widened her eyes alarmingly and she tensed, but he whispered to her, kissed her eyes closed, and never stopped for an instant. He found the place, and the pressure, that made her begin to sob and dig her nails into his hips. Then he smiled as he increased the rhythm and heard her cry out again and again with helpless delight.

It seemed hours before he finally gave in to his own need and shuddered against her in a culmination that exceeded his wildest dreams of fulfillment. He held her close, intimately joined to him, and fought to get enough air to breathe.

"Cataclysmic," he whispered into her throat. "That's what it was."

She was shivering, too, having experienced what the self-help articles referred to as "multiple culminations of pleasure."

"I never dreamed . . . !" she exclaimed breathlessly.

"Neither did I, sweetheart," he said heavily. "Neither did I."

He moved and rolled over, drawing her close against his side. They were both damp with sweat and pulsating in the aftermath of explosive satisfaction.

"Marge would kill us both," she began.

He chuckled. "Not likely. She's been busy on our behalf."

"Doing what?" she asked.

He ruffled her dark hair. "Sending out e-mailed invitations, calling caterers, ordering stuff. Which reminds me, I hope you're free Saturday. We're getting married at the ranch."

She sat up, gasping. "We're what?"

"Getting married," he replied slowly. "Why do you think I bought two rings?"

"But you've been swearing for years that you'd never get married!" Then she remembered why and her eyes went sad. "Because of that woman, the one you were going to marry," she said worriedly.

He drew her down beside him and looked at her solemnly. "When I was twenty-one, I fell in love. She was my exact opposite, and because my father opposed the marriage, I rebelled and ran headlong into it. She took the easy way out, rather than fighting him. You were right about that, although it hurt me to acknowledge it," he said quietly. "You'd have marched right up to my father and told him to do his worst." He smiled. "It's one of the things I love about you, that stubborn determination. She wasn't strong enough to stand up to him. So she killed herself. It would have been a disaster, if she hadn't," he added. "I'd have walked all over her, and she'd have been miserable. As things worked out, she saved her brother from prison and both of us from a bitter life together. I'm sorry it happened that way. I think she was mentally unstable. She was unhappy and she couldn't see a future without me. If she'd been able to talk to anyone about it, I don't think she'd have done it. I'll always regret what my father did, but he paid for it, in his way. So did I, unfortunately. Until you came along, and shook up my life, I didn't have much interest in living."

She felt happier, knowing that. She was sad for his fiancée, but she couldn't be sad that she'd ended up with J.B.

He traced her eyebrows, exploring her face, her soft body, with slow, tender tracings. "I never knew what love was, until you were eighteen. It was too soon, but I'd have married you then, if you'd been able to return what I felt for you."

Her arms closed around him. "It was too soon. I have a degree and I've had independence."

"And now?" he asked. "What about college?"

She drew in a slow, lazy breath. "You can always go back to college," she murmured. "I'd like to be with you for a few years. We might have a baby together and I'll be needed at home for a while. I can teach adult education at our community college if I get the urge. I only need a B.A. for that, and I've got it."

"We might have a baby together?" he teased, smiling. "How would that happen?"

She drew up one long leg and slid it gently over one of his. "We could do a lot more of what we've just done," she suggested, moving closer to him. "If we do it enough, who knows what might happen?"

He pursed his lips and moved between her legs.

"More of this, you mean?" he drawled, easing down.

"Definitely . . . more of this," she whispered unsteadily. She closed her eyes and tugged his mouth down over hers. Then she didn't speak again for a long, long time.

Twelve

Nell was overcome with delight when Tellie walked into Marge's house with J.B.'s arm around her. "You're back," she exclaimed to Tellie. "But what . . . how . . . why?"

J.B. lifted Tellie's left hand and extended it, with the diamond solitaire winking on her ring finger.

"Oh, my goodness!" Nell exclaimed, and hugged both of them with tearful enthusiasm. "Have you told Marge and the girls?" she asked.

"Marge is making all the arrangements for us," J.B. said with an ear-to-ear grin. "I'm sure she's told the girls. But it looks as if she was saving it as a surprise for you!"

"I can't believe it," Nell repeated, dabbing at her wet eyes. "I've never been so happy for anyone in my life! Have you had lunch?"

"Not yet," J.B. replied. "I thought we might have it with you, if that's all right?" he added with unexpected courtesy.

Nell's eyebrows went up. "Well! That's the first time you've ever treated me with any sort of courtesy."

"She's been working on me," he said, nodding toward Tellie.

"To good effect, apparently, too," Nell agreed. "I'm just floored!"

"Cook while you're getting adjusted," J.B. suggested. "I'm going to get Tellie's bag from her room and put it in the car. Marge packed it for her."

"Thanks," she said shyly, and not without a smile.

"How did you do it?" Nell asked when he was out of sight.

Tellie shook her head. "I have no idea. He showed up at the café where I was having coffee, and the next thing I knew, I was engaged. I thought he was involved with Bella."

"So did I," Nell agreed.

"But he wasn't," she replied, with a happy smile. "I went away thinking my life was over. Now look at me."

"I couldn't be happier for you," Nell said. "For both of you."

"So am I," Tellie told her. "In fact, I'm over the moon!"

Later, Marge and the girls came home, and all of them spent the evening going over wedding plans, because there wasn't much time.

J.B. drove Tellie to his house and installed her in the same guest bedroom he'd given her when she stayed with him during her bout of amnesia. They'd already decided that they'd abstain from any more sensual adventures until after the wedding, however old-fashioned it sounded.

The next day, J.B. bounced Tellie out of bed early.

"Get up, get up," he teased, lifting her free of the covers to kiss her with pure delight. "We're going shopping."

"You and me?" she asked, breathless.

He nodded, smiling. "You look pretty first thing in the morning."

"But I'm all rumpled and my hair isn't brushed."

He kissed her again, tenderly. "You're the most beautiful thing in my house, and in my heart," he whispered against her lips.

She kissed him back, sighing contentedly. She had the world in her arms, she thought. The whole world!

Albert fixed them croissants and strong coffee for breakfast, and J.B. privately lamented the lack of bacon and eggs and biscuits that Nell had always provided. Albert considered such a breakfast too heavy for normal people.

After breakfast, J.B. drove Tellie to a boutique in San Antonio to shop for a wedding gown.

"But you can't see it!" she insisted.

He glowered at her. "That's an old superstition!"

"Whether it is or not, you aren't looking," she said firmly. "Go get a cup of coffee and come back in an hour. Okay?"

He sighed irritably. "All right."

She reached up and kissed him sweetly. "I love you. Humor me."

He stopped glowering and smiled. "Headache," he accused.

"I'll make it all up to you. I promise."

He bent and brushed his mouth over her closed eye-lids. "You already have. Everything!"

She hugged him close. "Go away."

He laughed, winking as he left her to go down the street toward a nearby Starbucks shop.

The owner of the boutique gave her a wicked grin. "You manage him very well."

"I do, don't I? But he doesn't know I'm doing it, and we're not going to tell him. Deal?"

"Deal! Now let me show you what I've got in your size . . ."

Tellie ended up with a gloriously embroidered gown with cape sleeves, a tight waist, a vee neckline and an exquisite long train, also embroidered. The veil was held in place by jeweled combs and fell to the waist in front. It was the most beautiful gown she'd ever seen, and it suited her nice tan.

"I love it," Tellie told the owner. "It's a dream of a wedding gown."

"It looks lovely on you," came the satisfied reply. "Now for the accessories!"

By the time J.B. came back, the gown and accessories were all neatly boxed and ready to carry out.

"Did you get something pretty?" he asked.

"Something beautiful," Tellie told him, smiling.

"I wish you'd let me pay for it," he said as they drove home. "I'd have taken you to Neiman Marcus."

"What I got is lovely," she said, "and one of a kind.

The owner of the boutique is a designer in her own right. You'll see. It's going to make a stir."

He clasped her hand tight in his own. "You'll make the stir, sweetheart. You're lovely."

She gave him an odd look, and his jaw tautened.

"I didn't mean it, Tellie," he said quietly. "I was ashamed and frustrated and I took it all out on you. I wanted you so much. I thought you'd never be able to feel desire for me. It made me cruel."

"Maybe if you'd tried a little harder," she pointed out, "it wouldn't have taken me so long."

He sighed. "Leave it to you to put your finger on a nerve and push," he said philosophically. "Yes, I should have. But I was still living in the past, afraid of being devastated again by love. It wasn't until Grange came along, and cauterized the wound, that I realized I was using the past as an excuse. Maybe I sensed that it was going to be different with you."

"I can see why you were reluctant," she said. Her hand tightened in his. "But I'd never hurt you, J.B. I love you too much."

"Thank God for that," he said, sighing contentedly. He smiled. "You'll never get away from me, Tellie."

"I'll never want to." She meant it, too.

The wedding was a small, private one, but two reporters with cameramen showed up, and so did Grange, resplendent in a blue vested suit. He looked very different from the cowboy Tellie had dated. The Ballengers were there, also, with their wives, and of course

198

Marge and Dawn and Brandi and Nell. Even Albert put on a suit and gave Tellie away.

Tellie couldn't see much of J.B. as she walked down the aisle with her veil neatly in place. But when she got to the altar, she was shocked, delighted and amused to see what he was wearing with his suit. It was one of the ties—the gaudy, green-and-gold dragon tie that she'd given him for every single birthday and Christmas for years. She had to force herself not to laugh. But she didn't miss his wink.

When the minister pronounced them man and wife, he turned and lifted her veil, and the look on his face was the most profound she'd ever seen. He smiled, tenderly, and bent and kissed her with soft, sweet reverence.

Nell and Marge cried. The girls sighed. Tellie pressed close into J.B.'s arms and just hugged him, feeling radiant and happier than she'd ever been in her life. He hugged her back, sighing contentedly.

"I suppose the best man won," Grange mused at the reception Albert and the caterers had prepared in the ballroom at the ranch.

"I guess he did," J.B. replied, with a forced smile.

"She's very special," the other man said quietly. "But it was always you, and I always knew it. I'm a bad marriage risk."

"I thought I was, too," J.B. replied. He looked toward Tellie with his heart in his eyes. "But maybe I'm not."

Grange just laughed, and lifted his champagne glass in a toast.

"How'd you come out at the court-martial?" J.B. asked.

Grange grinned. "He got five years. I got a commendation and the offer of reinstatement."

"Are you going to take them up on it?"

Grange shrugged. "I don't know yet. I'll have to think about it. I've had another offer. I'm thinking it over."

"One that involves staying here?" J.B. asked shrewdly.

"Yes." He met the other man's gaze. "Is that going to be a problem."

J.B. smiled wryly. "Not now that Tellie's married to me," he drawled.

Grange laughed. "Just checking."

J.B. sipped champagne. "The past is over," he said. "We can't change it. All we can do is live with it. I loved your sister. I'm sorry things worked out the way they did."

"She was a sad person," the other man replied solemnly. "It wasn't the first time she'd thought about taking her own life. There were two other times, both connected with men she thought didn't want her."

J.B. looked shocked.

Grange grimaced. "Sorry. Maybe I shouldn't have said anything. But in the long run, you're better off with the truth. She was emotionally shattered, since childhood. She went to a psychiatrist when she was in high school for counseling, because she slashed her wrists."

"I didn't know," J.B. ground out.

"Neither did I until my father was dying, and told me everything. He said my mother had always worried that suicide would end my sister's life. She couldn't handle stress at all. It's nothing against her. Some people are born not being able to cope with life."

"I suppose they are," J.B. said, and he was remembering Tellie, and how she would have handled the same opposition from his father.

Grange clapped J.B. on the shoulder. "Go dance with your wife. Let the past bury itself. Life goes on. I hope both of you will be very happy. And I mean that."

J.B. shook his hand. "Thanks. You can come to dinner sometimes. As long as you don't bring roses," he added dryly.

Grange burst out laughing.

That night, Albert went to see his brother for the weekend, and Tellie and J.B. spent lazy, delicious hours trying out new ways to express their love for each other in his big king-size bed.

She was shivering and pouring sweat and gasping when they finally stopped long enough to sip cold champagne.

"I just didn't read enough books," she said breathlessly.

He grinned. "Good thing I did."

She laughed, curling close to his hairy chest. "Don't brag."

"I don't need to. Will you be able to walk tomorrow?"

"Hobble, maybe," she murmured sleepily. "I'm so tired . . . !"

He bent and kissed her eyelids shut. "You're magnificent."

"So are you," she said, kissing his chest.

He took the champagne glass away, put it on the table along with his own and stroked her hair. "Tellie?"

"Hmm?"

"I hope you want kids right away."

"Hmm."

He drew in a lazy breath and closed his eyes. "That had better be a yes, because we forgot to think about precautions."

She didn't answer. He didn't worry. She'd already made her stand on children very clear. He figured he'd get used to fatherhood. It would be as natural as making love to Tellie. And *that* he seemed to do to perfection, he thought, as he glanced down at her satisfied, dreamy expression.

"It's just indecent, that's what it is," Marge groaned as she and Tellie went shopping at the mall outside Jacobsville. She glowered at the younger woman. "I mean, honestly, J.B. didn't have to be so impatient!"

"It was a mutual impatience," Tellie pointed out with a grin, "and I'm happier than I ever dreamed I could be."

"Yes, but Tellie, you've just been married two weeks!"

"I noticed."

Marge shook her head. "J.B.'s strutting already. You shouldn't let him send you on errands like this. I mean, things do go wrong, sometimes . . ."

"They won't this time," Tellie said dreamily. "I'm as sure of it as I've ever been of anything. Besides," she added with a grin, "tell me you aren't excited."

Marge grimaced. "Well, I am, but . . ."

"No buts," Tellie said firmly. "We just take one day at a time and enjoy it. Hi, Chief!" she broke off to greet their police chief. "How's it going?"

"Life is beautiful," Cash Grier said with a grin.

"We heard that Tippy laid a frying pan across the skull of her would-be assassin," Marge said, digging gently.

"She did. And have you seen the tabloid story about it, by any chance?" he asked them, and his dark eyes twinkled.

"The one that says you're getting married soon?" Tellie teased.

"That's the one. In fact, we're getting married tomorrow." He chuckled. "I'm not going to let her get away now!"

"Congratulations," Tellie told him. "I hope you'll both be as happy as J.B. and I are."

"We're going to be," he said with assurance. "I expect to grow old fighting what little crime I can dig up here in Jacobsville. In between, Tippy may make a movie or two before we start our family."

Tellie put a hand on her belly. "J.B. and I already have started," she said, smiling from ear to ear. "The blood test came back positive just yesterday."

He whistled. "You two don't waste time, do you? You've only been married two weeks!"

"We were sort of in a hurry," Tellie chuckled.

"A flaming rush," Marge added. "And now we're out prematurely buying maternity clothes, do you believe it?"

"That's the spirit," Cash said. "If you've got it, flaunt it, I always say."

He went on toward his squad car, and Tellie dragged Marge into the maternity shop.

Three months later, J.B. came in looking like two miles of rough road. He was wet and muddy and his chaps were as caked as his shirt. But when he saw Tellie in her maternity pants and blouse, all the weariness went out of his face.

He chuckled, catching her by the waist. "I love the way that looks," he said, and bent to kiss her. "I'm all muddy," he murmured when she tried to move closer. "We don't want to mess up that pretty outfit. Tell you what, I'll clean up and we'll call Marge and the girls and go out for a nice supper. How about that?"

She hesitated, looking guilty. "Well . . ."

His eyebrows arched. "Is something wrong?" he asked, suddenly worried.

"It's not that."

"Then, what?"

"So you're finally home!" came a stringent voice from the direction of the kitchen. Nell came out, wearing a dirty apron and carrying a big spoon. "I made you chicken and dumplings, homemade rolls and a congealed fruit salad," she announced with a smile.

J.B. drew in a sharp breath. "You're back? For good?" he asked hopefully.

"For good," she said. "I have to take care of Tellie and make sure she eats right. Marge is getting some help of her own, so it isn't as if I'm leaving her in the lurch. And I gave her Albert. Is that okay?" she added worriedly.

"Thank God!" he exclaimed. "I didn't have the heart to let him go, but I'm damned tired of French cooking! All I want is meat and potatoes. And apple pie," he added.

"I made one," Nell said. "Albert likes Marge, and the girls love his cooking. They're of an age to like parties. So, all our problems are solved. Right?"

He grinned. "Most of them, anyway. I'll get cleaned up and we'll have a romantic dinner for . . ."

"Six," Nell informed him.

"Six?" he exclaimed.

Tellie moved close to him and reached up to kiss his dirt-smudged cheek. "I invited Marge and the girls over for chicken and dumplings. It will be romantic, though, I promise. We'll have lots of candles."

He laughed, shaking his head. "Okay. An intimate little romantic dinner for six." He kissed her back. "I love you," he said.

She smiled. "I love you back."

He went upstairs and Nell sighed. "I never thought

205

I'd see the boss look like that," she told Tellie. "What a change!"

"I inspire him," Tellie mused. "And while I'm inspiring, I'd really like to remodel that frilly pink bedroom and make a nursery out of it."

Nell wriggled her eyebrows. "Count on me as a coconspirator. I'll be in the kitchen."

Tellie watched her go. She looked toward the staircase, where J.B. had disappeared. So much pain, she thought, had led to so much pleasure. Perhaps life did balance the two after all. She knew that she'd been so happy. J.B. and a baby, too. Only a few months before, she'd been agonizing over a lonely, cold future. Now she was married, and pregnant, and her husband loved her obsessively. It was a dream come true.

She turned and followed Nell into the kitchen. Life, she thought dreamily, was sweet.

Later, she spared a thought for that poor young woman who'd died so tragically years ago, and for Grange, who'd paid a high price for his illegal activities. She hoped Grange would find his own happiness one day. He'd gone to D.C., but was planning to come back and do something a little more adventurous than working for the Ballengers, but he didn't mention what it was. He'd sent her a post-card telling her that, with his new address. J.B. had seen the card, and murmured that he hoped Tellie wasn't planning any future contact with Grange. She assured him that she hadn't any such plans, and kissed him so enthusiastically that very soon he forgot Grange altogether.

• • •

Marge and the girls were happy about the baby, and Marge was finally in the best of health on her new medicines. Tellie was relieved that she continued to improve.

That night, while J.B. slept, Tellie sat and watched his lean, hard face, wiped clean of expression, and thought how very lucky she was. He wasn't perfect, but he was certainly Tellie's dream of perfection. She bent and very softly kissed his chiseled mouth.

His dark eyes slid open and twinkled. "Don't waste kisses, sweetheart," he whispered, and reached up to draw her down into his warm, strong arms. "They're precious."

"Yours certainly are," she whispered back, and she smiled contentedly against his mouth.

"Yours, too," he murmured.

She closed her eyes and thought of a happy future, where they'd be surrounded by children and, later, grandchildren. They'd grow old together, safe in the cocoon of their love for each other, with a lifetime of memories to share. And this, Tellie thought with delight, was only the beginning of it all! Her arms tightened around J.B. Life was sweeter than her dreams had ever been. Sweeter than them all.

Center Point Publishing
600 Brooks Road ● PO Box 1
Thorndike ME 04986-0001 USA

(207) 568-3717

US & Canada:
1 800 929-9108